DARK OBSESSION

Seven years ago Francesco Mazzoni told Kate Thompson exactly what he thought of her — she was a gold-digger. Kate has come across men like Francesco before. Rich, powerful and ruthless — for him, everything comes down to money. But some things can't be bought, and Kate is out to prove that she's one of them. No-one could be more shocked than Kate when a terrific physical attraction suddenly begins to blaze between her and this darkly handsome and wickedly dangerous man . . .

LISA ANDREWS

DARK OBSESSION

Complete and Unabridged

LINFORD
Leicester

First published in Great Britain in 2001

First Linford Edition
published 2004

British Library CIP Data

Andrews, Lisa
    Dark obsession.—Large print ed.—
    Linford romance library
    1. Single parents—England—Fiction
    2. Love stories
    3. Large type books
    I. Title
    823.9'14 [F]

    ISBN 1–84395–118–5

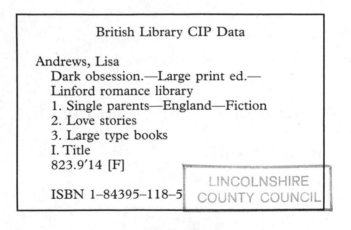

Published by
F. A. Thorpe (Publishing)
Anstey, Leicestershire

Set by Words & Graphics Ltd.
Anstey, Leicestershire
Printed and bound in Great Britain by
T. J. International Ltd., Padstow, Cornwall

This book is printed on acid-free paper

1

Kate leaped up the stairs two at a time. No mean feat in her close-fitting business suit and three-inch heels. Tamworth Textiles was on the third floor. It could have been worse, she supposed, as she paused for a quick slug of breath on the second. And she could have gambled on the lift getting her there quicker, but the crowd of people waiting for it suggested otherwise. She'd hardened up a lot in the past few years, but not to the extent of battering people out of the way. Not even in an emergency!

'Kate Thompson. Sorry I'm late.' That was all she could manage before she needed to draw breath again. After all this, she hoped that she'd still be given an interview. Hoped that running full pelt along Oxford Street, trying to dodge the tourists who probably thought she was a shoplifter, hadn't all been in vain.

The receptionist assessed her coolly. 'I tried ringing your mobile,' she stated.

Kate fished the offending article out of her bag. 'I tried ringing you as well.'

'We have several lines,' said the woman in a voice that informed Kate that as an excuse this rated as pitiful.

'No, I meant that the battery was dead.'

'Indeed?' said the woman in the tone of one who would never venture out without a spare battery in her handbag.

Kate felt the job sliding away. In desperation, she decided to appeal to the woman's softer side. 'It's my son, you see. He loves playing with the ring tones on it . . . ' Her voice trailed away. Something . . . maybe it was the shudder which the woman gave at the mention of a child — told her that she was wasting her time.

'I was going to tell you that your interview will be at least an hour late.'

The receptionist looked pointedly at her watch. 'However, you shouldn't have too long to wait now.'

The sarcasm wasn't lost on her, but Kate smiled sweetly. She was still in with a chance!

'Coffee?'

At last, a spark of humanity.

'Thanks. I could kill for one.'

'Hardly necessary.' She walked away before Kate could decide whether the tone was humorous or sarcastic. Giving up, she sat down and scanned the company magazine for snippets to throw into her interview.

Her eyes glazed. Surely the only readers of this magazine were people like her, hoping to impress at interviews?

Through a glass partition, Kate could hear the sound of a male voice. It had only just penetrated her consciousness, but she realised it had been there all the time — strong, cultured, and very angry. The person on the receiving end was getting the dressing-down of a lifetime. Kate grimaced. Maybe she should take notice of the signs and go home now.

Unfortunately, she couldn't afford that luxury. Couldn't afford any luxury, as it happened. The bank and building society letters were quite clear on that point. So if there was still a chance of this job, she had to give it her best effort.

She shifted in her chair and gazed through the frosted glass, hoping for something that might help in her forth-coming interview. All she gained was the impression of a tall, suited, dark-haired man, and the muffled sounds of anger. A lot of help!

She swivelled back in her chair as she heard footsteps. At least the receptionist's arrival was preceded by a welcoming aroma of freshly-brewed coffee. Things were looking up.

'Thanks.' Kate took a sip immediately. Blue Mountain, if she wasn't mistaken. Lovely.

'Mr Mazzoni may yet be some time,'

said the woman, and Kate nearly choked on it.

'Are you all right?' asked the receptionist, slapping her hard on the back.

Kate struggled for breath. 'I'm sorry, who did you say would be interviewing me?' It couldn't be him. This company was owned by an Elizabeth Webster. It had absolutely nothing to do with the Mazzoni empire. She'd done her homework. She always did.

'Mr Mazzoni,' said the woman, and then, 'Mr Francesco Mazzoni,' in case there was any doubt.

Sparks of light flashed before her, the room danced, and a cold dampness formed over her body, but somehow Kate struggled to her feet.

'May I use the ladies' room?' she asked in a voice that she hardly recognised as her own.

The startled woman pointed her in the right direction and, seconds later, Kate shut the door behind her. But she couldn't shut out the nightmare that had resurfaced. With shaking hands, she splashed her face with water in a futile attempt to quell the rising tide of nausea.

How could she have let this happen? Since that terrible night when Nico had drowned, she'd tracked his brother's activities with a vigilance bordering on obsession. His cruelty had almost destroyed her, but she'd survived. More importantly, Nico's child had survived. There were countless reasons she didn't want to face Mazzoni again, but number one was Dominic's safety.

The thought of her son spurred her into action. She had to get out of here. She'd plead sickness. A quick glance at the ghost-like reflection in the mirror reassured her that this wouldn't be too difficult.

Pausing only to wipe away mascara smears with a tissue and brushing away the blonde strands that clung to her face, Kate headed for the door.

Lord, why hadn't she noticed? Hadn't everything conspired to prevent her coming here today? She shuddered as she recalled the chain of events that had made her late. And even when she got here, why hadn't she recognised Mazzoni's voice? Wasn't he in top form, bullying some poor unfortunate as he'd once bullied her?

Busy composing excuses as she walked towards the receptionist's desk, Kate wasn't immediately aware of the dark presence standing beside it.

She was too late!

As she took in the stern, imposing figure of Francesco Mazzoni, Kate froze, and waited for recognition to dawn on his chiselled features. He stared at her for a lifetime, the only sound the slight drumming of his fingers on the receptionist's desk.

At last he opened his mouth to speak but, 'You are very pale, Miss Thompson. Are you ill?' was all he said.

Kate stared at him. The bastard hadn't recognised her! Never, in all the nightmare scenarios she'd played out in her imagination, had this eventuality occurred to her. Seven years ago, he'd demonstrated that she was less than nothing to his family. Now he was doing it all over again. The minute he'd stormed out of the cottage she'd shared with Nico, he must have forgotten all about her existence.

That knowledge shot such a blaze of anger through her that Kate had to look away.

'Are you ill, Miss Thompson?' he repeated, this time with more than an edge of irritation to his voice.

'I'm fine,' she spat.

She would be. Slowly it dawned on her that after all this time she was finally safe. She was standing only inches from the man yet he hadn't a clue that they'd met before. There was no way that the Mazzonis would ever discover Dominic's existence. Francesco wouldn't be remotely interested in any child of hers.

'Whatever you say.' Francesco held open the door to his office. She obeyed the gesture and walked in, belatedly realising that she'd blown her illness excuse.

'What a day!' He swept the files on the desk to one side while she located the seat opposite and sank into it, her mind racing through further ways of getting out of this interview.

'Do sit down,' he said pointedly.

Kate crossed her legs and waited. Perhaps she needn't worry. Francesco was hardly likely to appoint someone with such bad manners and evident animosity towards him, even as a temporary secretary.

She stared at him coldly, noting that the boils and warts she'd wished on him had failed to materialise. His skin was smooth, tanned, and unblemished. Not only had he been first in the queue when they'd been doling out worldly riches, he'd also pushed his way to the front when they were giving out looks as well.

Mocha-brown eyes met her light blue ones directly, and Kate's heart slammed in her chest. It was uncanny the genetic trait that Nico, Dominic and Francesco shared that made them look so similar. It was the eyes mainly, and it disturbed her deeply that she'd looked with adoration into the first two, yet with such utter loathing into the third.

'I presume the agency explained the situation?'

'Yes.' Kate tightened her grip on her fingers as practicalities assailed her. The agency. She couldn't afford to alienate them. After cancelling a job when Dominic had chicken pox, she had the feeling that she'd been given a final warning. Not getting this job might be OK with them. Not getting this job, with Mazzoni phoning to enquire what the hell had possessed them to send her, would definitely not.

'Due to my permanent secretary's illness, I need a bilingual secretary to accompany me to Birmingham tomorrow and Friday. Apparently you fit the description.' The glance he threw her suggested it was beyond his comprehension how they'd ever come to that conclusion. So far so good.

'Before we begin, however, perhaps you could tell me why you were so late for our meeting today?' Unaccountably, he smiled, and a stunned Kate watched the harsh lines of his face melt, until she realised that the smile wasn't meant for her. It was directed at the receptionist who was bringing in a tray of coffee. The same woman who must have dropped her in it regarding her late arrival.

'Thank you, Mrs Blanchard.' He took the tray and turned back to her. 'Coffee?' A trace of the smile still smouldered at the corner of his lips.

'Thanks.' She hadn't tasted much of the last one. To her surprise, he poured a cup for her, but what was more surprising was the evident enjoyment with which he drank his own. Nico had always poured scorn on the British habit of drinking coffee throughout the day and especially hers of drinking it after meals as well. He had drunk two cups of bitumen-strength coffee to wake him up in the morning, then refused to drink another drop for the rest of the day. Somehow she would have expected his brother to be the same.

'We were discussing the reason for your lateness,' he prompted her.

Kate sighed. 'Some guy decided to end it all on the Central Line.'

Francesco's head shot up and he studied her closely. Surely he didn't believe that she'd make up a thing like that? She stared back at him, disgusted.

Carefully he replaced his cup on the saucer. 'Selfish man,' he murmured.

'What?'

His eyes narrowed as they registered the tone of her voice. 'I said that the man was selfish,' he repeated.

It took all of Kate's self control not to reach over and slap him. She couldn't begin to comprehend the anguish of a mind that wanted to end its existence, yet all this creep could say was that he was selfish. 'Poor man!' she contradicted.

Francesco raised his eyebrows. 'His death seems to have affected you a great deal.'

And what was so surprising about that? 'Too right, it has,' she said and felt a stab of conscience. Since arriving at Tamworth Textiles, the shock of the morning's events had faded somewhat.

Francesco wasn't finished. 'Then consider how it must have affected the driver of your train and tell me again that the man was not selfish.'

Kate shrugged, unwilling to concede anything to this man. 'I don't suppose he thought about the driver when he jumped,' she murmured but Francesco, knowing that he'd won the argument, had already lost interest.

'Time is passing, Miss Thompson,' he said, glancing at his watch. If it is agreeable to you I will conduct the remainder of this interview in Italian.' And without waiting for her assent, he launched into his mother tongue as if he were entering a speed-talking competition.

Kate's senses reeled. Out of all the Italians she'd worked for, not one had ever spoken this fast. Nobody did! And it was so obvious why he was doing it. He'd already decided not to appoint her, and now he was looking for the reason. Well, tough! He could cite any other reason he wanted apart from her professional ability. She was good at this, and she wouldn't have her reputation slurred by him.

And just as she'd settled into his rhythm and was answering him almost as rapidly as he was firing the questions, Francesco changed tack. He began speaking in Roman dialect, dropping the end of his words as Nico used to do. At first it was a shock, and she must have stared at him open-mouthed until her determination that he wouldn't beat her kicked in and she adapted to the challenge. Thank you, Nico. If he hadn't insisted on speaking his language rather than hers, she wouldn't have had a hope of following his brother.

By the time he raised a neatly-manicured hand to stop her, Kate felt as though she was functioning on hyper-drive. She watched in amazement as the stern expression relaxed into a broad smile. 'Oh, you are good, Miss Thompson. You are very good,' he chuckled, and she could only stare, mesmerised, as the black depths of his eyes shimmered like warm coals.

'You must forgive me. My acquaintance said it was so, but I had to check for myself. But I am curious how you are able to speak my language so well?' He opened a folder and traced his finger down a sheet of paper. She realised, to her horror, that it was her CV. It contained no lies, but the truth was well-hidden.

'Hard work, dedication . . . '

'Evidently.' He looked at her. 'Tell me, Miss Thompson, have you ever visited Rome?'

The question felt like a punch in the stomach. It had been her greatest wish to visit Rome, to attend her lover's burial there, but the man sitting before her had refused it and left her in no doubt what he thought her motives were for wanting to meet Nico's family.

'No,' she gasped, her throat as dry as sand.

'Then you were taught Italian by a Roman.' It was a statement rather than a question. Luckily, Francesco hadn't noticed her distress. He'd been too busy reading her CV, and the frown creasing his brow suggested he hadn't been overly impressed by it.

When he looked at her again, she'd regained her composure. It was almost over. He'd found what he'd been looking for in her CV, and this was the part where he told her, 'Don't call us, we'll call you.' She did her best to form an expression of suitable regret.

Francesco leaned back in his chair, his fingers linked behind his head. 'To be frank, Miss Thompson, I didn't think you would suit, but time is of the essence and your linguistic skill is exceptional.'

Kate's heart began to beat more quickly. Surely that backhanded compliment didn't mean what she thought it meant?

'Now, if you'll excuse me for a moment, I need to make one phone call and then we shall discuss arrangements for tomorrow.' He rose to his feet and left the room as the predicament she was in finally sunk in. She'd landed the job!

A job she didn't want.

And all because she'd been too stubborn to let him make a fool of her speaking his language.

Cursing to herself, she reached for the pot of coffee. It was now cold, but she needed the caffeine it contained. She needed something. She needed her head examined!

What had possessed her to acquit herself in such a fashion? He'd more or less told her that she hadn't a hope in hell of getting the job before that.

Pride. Stupid pride. He'd wiped the floor with her seven years ago, and her self-respect had refused to allow him to do it again.

But what was the use of self-respect when it got you into a mess like this? She gulped down her coffee. It was foul, but she poured another cup. She needed something to jump-start her brain. It was exhausted from its recent exertions and was insisting on having a rest.

What were her options?

She could tell Mazzoni she'd changed her mind and didn't want the position.

He would go ballistic. Even someone with his contacts would find it virtually impossible to get someone else by tomorrow. If he'd been able to, they'd already have been here and she'd have been competing against them. That was why he was paying well over the odds for the job. That was why she had been prepared to leave Dominic with her parents in order to take it.

Hell! Kate rapped her knuckles against the side of the table until pain forced her to stop. There didn't seem to be any options left. One only needed a brief acquaintance with Francesco to know that he'd make damned sure that she never worked as an interpreter again if she crossed him now.

Dominic's trusting face entered her mind and Kate sighed heavily. There really was only one option. She might have believed in her youth that all you needed was love, but she was more realistic now. She might love her son so much that it hurt, but she also had a duty to provide for him.

So what was the problem? That's what Nico would have said. He always laughed at her for worrying about things. Kate wrinkled her brow. Was she wrong? Was she imagining dangers where there were none?

She decided to look at things differently. Francesco hadn't recognised her; it was only for two days, and she'd earn enough to keep the bank and building society off her back for some time.

The conclusion was self-evident: take the job and keep her feelings for the man in check.

Kate brushed a shaking hand through her hair. Could it *really* be that simple?

2

Francesco Mazzoni re-entered the room
before she'd come to any clear conclusion. 'The day is panning out
better than I had hoped.' He smiled
cryptically.

Kate decided he was referring to his
phone call rather than to her, but
bravely tugged her lips in the semblance
of a smile. That wasn't too bad. Her
face hadn't actually cracked with the
effort. Maybe she could do this, after
all?

He squeezed past her as he made
for his seat and the slight citrus smell
of his aftershave tickled her nostrils.
Something else, less definable, tingled
her arm where he'd brushed against
her, and she automatically rubbed
the sleeve of her jacket to rid herself
of the sensation. Damn! He'd seen
her. The smile vanished and he

looked at her strangely.

'This material picks up every piece of fluff,' she murmured, picking an imaginary thread off her other sleeve. It seemed to satisfy him.

'Let me run through the arrangements,' he said, and she tried to follow his instructions. This was happening. With the exception of being run over by a bus on the way home, she couldn't think how to stop it now.

'You will arrive here at eleven o'clock tomorrow morning. Please don't be late. I wish to be in Birmingham by mid-afternoon. This may prove fruitless. Roberto cannot always arrive so early but, when he does, he likes to play several games of squash before dinner and I, of course, like to accommodate him.' He gave a self-mocking gesture but Kate, unable to believe that this man would put himself out for anyone, failed to respond.

He sighed, picked up a pencil and tapped it lightly on the table. 'This meeting is important, Miss Thompson.

I will do everything in my power to ensure that it is a success.'

'Of course.' Kate, feeling like a reprimanded child, began to flush. Without trying at all, this man still had the power to intimidate her. It was only for two days, she reminded herself, then repeated it silently over and over like a mantra. She could do this. She had to.

But why was she blushing? Good Lord, she hadn't done that for years. Her cheeks stung as she forced herself to look up and into midnight-black eyes that crinkled at the edges. She ought to have known he was the type to be amused by another's discomfort.

His eyes flickered over her face and down her neck to the opening of her blouse where the flesh, she knew without needing to look in a mirror, was streaked with pink.

'Your services shouldn't be required before dinner.' He glanced away and reverted to his pencil tapping, and Kate's skin reverted to its normal paleness. Thank goodness he had little interest in her. His eyes were like lasers as they grazed over her, stripping the top layer of skin bare. She knew it was their past history that was making her hypersensitive to him, but it was still deeply disturbing.

'Roberto and Elena are old family friends, which is the reason for the social evening before business proper the following day. Elena . . . ' He paused, and the lasers conducted another circuit over her body.

Elena what? she wondered, steeling herself against their probing.

'Elena . . . ' again there was a slight hesitation, 'is a very nice lady.'

Elena is clearly a pain of the highest order, she translated. Nothing that she wouldn't expect of a close friend of Francesco Mazzoni.

'She and my permanent secretary are very good friends.'

As she'd never met Francesco's permanent secretary, that information was meaningless. Maybe his secretary was a pain of the second highest order, and that was why they got on so well . . . ?

'Although Thursday evening will be a social occasion, it will also be a formal one. You will need to wear an evening dress and . . . ' The rest of his instructions were lost as Kate concentrated on the latest problem. Where on earth was she going to conjure up an evening dress before tomorrow morning? Maybe his permanent secretary had racks of the things she could slip on at a moment's notice, but nobody had ever asked her to wear one before. The last film premiere she'd attended had been in her dreams.

'There is a problem?'

Houston we have a problem! 'No,' she said, as her brain once again raced though various options.

'Tell me what the problem is,' he commanded.

'It's OK, I can hire one,' she said as the solution presented itself. A quick flick through Yellow Pages, get up at the crack of dawn tomorrow, and she was sorted.

'Hire what?'

'An evening dress.' What did he think?

'Oh.' He gave her a quizzical look. 'You don't possess one?'

'No.' She was tempted to say that she was bored with the ones stuffed in her wardrobe, but instead she stared back at him levelly. *Welcome to the real world, pal, where feeding and clothing your child come way before designer dresses.*

He seemed unable to meet her gaze. 'Forgive my insensitivity,' he murmured, pulled a fountain pen from the inside pocket of his suit. She watched as he scrawled something on a sheet of paper and raised her eyebrows as he handed her the note. If this was a recommendation as to where she could obtain suitable clothing, he could forget it. She wasn't about to blow her whole pay packet on one dress.

'I have an account here,' he

explained. 'Please choose a suitable dress, mention my name, and everything will be taken care of.'

Kate shook her head. She'd only ever wanted one thing from Francesco Mazzoni. His compassion. After he'd refused that and wiped the floor with her, she never wanted another thing from him again.

'Please don't argue, Miss Thompson. As an employer, I have specified that you need to wear certain clothing to undertake your duties. Therefore, as an employer, it is beholden on me to provide it. Think of it as a uniform.'

Kate bit her lip. No way. The sales staff would think she was his mistress if she turned up demanding an evening dress. 'I'd rather hire,' she said quietly.

Francesco rose to his feet. For a second Kate thought he intended to hit her, but instead he walked across the room, stuffed his hands into his trouser pockets and gazed out of the window.

'I have already mentioned how important this occasion is.' His voice was low but precise. 'I would much prefer it if you wore a new dress.'

It was as well that Francesco continued gazing out of the window. An arrow of hatred shot from Kate, sliced easily through the soft wool of his suit, penetrated his backbone, and pierced his heart. So that was it! He didn't trust her not to turn up in some shabby second-hand frock. The occasion was far too important for that!

'Do I have your agreement?' He turned back to her and Kate struggled to hide her contempt.

'It's your money,' she said, not altogether succeeding.

For a second, his eyes widened in surprise. 'I'll take that as a 'yes',' he said, returning to his desk.

★ ★ ★

Kate was not late the next day. Anxious, guilty and frazzled when she arrived back at Tamworth Textiles, but not late. Anxious because of the prospect of two days in Francesco Mazzoni's company, guilty because of leaving her son, and frazzled because of Dominic's performance that morning.

She knew, just knew that the tummy ache he complained of was a product of his imagination. He was a sensitive child who had picked up on her own unease. However, that didn't stop her worrying about him. The way he'd clung to her when she took him to school had been heart-breaking. She'd hung around long after she should, just to make sure he was settled, and only when she saw him laughing and behaving normally did she leave and run to the tube.

She worried also that Dominic was becoming too much for her parents to cope with. They welcomed him at any time, but it was less than a year since her dad's heart attack, and she felt that her mum had enough to do looking after him.

Kate took a deep breath before punching the lift button for the third floor. Maybe she should try writing a best-seller — 'Women Who Worry Too Much'. She grimaced as the lift doors opened and she prepared herself to meet Mazzoni again. Yep, she was a leading authority on that!

'Don't be late.' Wasn't that what he'd said yesterday? Wasn't that why she'd hurried around London, lugging her suitcase behind her all morning? In case she didn't make it on time?

But at least forty-five minutes waiting outside his office, listening to the deep resonant voice and glimpsing his profile through the glass, allowed her to accustom herself once more to being in Francesco Mazzoni's presence.

At least that was what she thought before he eventually strode out, smiling broadly. 'Sorry,' he said, though he didn't look sorry at all. But that wasn't what affected her, what caused her stomach to lurch strangely. It was his manner. The relaxed, thoroughly-pleased-with-himself way in which he walked towards her was so reminiscent of his brother that she closed her eyes momentarily to rid herself of it. The cold, off-hand Francesco Mazzoni she could cope with. The new, improved version was more difficult.

'Derek is waiting for us downstairs,' he said, though she didn't have a clue who Derek was. Should she? Had her brain turned to jelly? She made to pick up her suitcase, but he was too quick for her. With his briefcase in one hand and her suitcase in the other, he was making for the stairs before she'd scrambled out of her seat.

He turned to wait for her and, despite herself, Kate started to laugh.

'What?' His brow creased into a frown.

Kate surveyed the man before her. Immaculately groomed, in a well-cut Italian suit and tastefully contrasting tie and shirt. In one hand he was carrying an expensive leather briefcase and in the other a catalogue surplus suitcase.

'You'll have to lose the suitcase.' She

grinned. 'It doesn't go with your image.'

He glanced at the case, but remained holding it. 'And what exactly is my image, Kate?' he enquired.

The use of her Christian name was like a slap. It sobered her immediately. 'Expensive,' she said, and continued down the stairs.

Parked on double yellow lines outside the office building was a bottle green Bentley. It had to belong to Mazzoni. As did the uniformed chauffeur that was standing beside it.

Kate pursed her lips. Great! They were going to drive to Birmingham with people pointing at them all the way. Francesco set down her case by her feet.

'Like I said . . . ' She gestured to the car.

'Expensive,' Francesco murmured, his lips curving into a smile. She'd meant the word as an insult but he seemed to have taken it as a compliment. 'But don't you agree that it's the most wonderful car?' He reached out and trailed his fingertips over the bodywork as though he were stroking a woman.

'Not much cop for parking at Sainsbury's,' she retorted, needing to dispel the sensuality of the gesture. What was it about the Mazzonis and cars? Nico had worked his way through a Rover, a Jaguar, and a Porsche in the eighteen months in which she'd known him, and his son must have the largest collection of die-cast models of any six year-old in London.

Francesco was laughing. 'You have an amusing turn of phrase, Kate.'

Kate stiffened. What was this with her Christian name? She didn't normally mind people using it. But not him. Yesterday, it had been 'Miss Thompson'. That was fine. It felt like a barrier between them. She was sure that he wouldn't be too thrilled if she started calling him Francesco. No, she was certain that he wouldn't like that at all.

She glanced at the man she presumed must be Derek as he picked up her case to put it in the boot. If his boss hadn't noticed its cheapness then his employee certainly had. She almost expected him to refuse to load it, the expression of distaste on his face was so great.

Kate sighed. Two days, she reminded herself once more, as she stepped into the car. Two days before she could return to normality and to her son, who didn't mind what kind of suitcase she had so long as she gave him regular hugs, played with him, and read him a bedtime story every night.

The car purred away from the pavement attracting, as she'd expected, several interested stares. What a pity she couldn't trade places with Dominic for five minutes. He'd have given a year's pocket money for such an experience, whereas she couldn't care less what form of transport they took to Birmingham so long as they arrived there in one piece.

Francesco caught her smile, misinterpreted it, and smiled back. '*Che bella!*' He gestured at the understated elegance of the interior.

Kate gave a tight smile back. If you say so, she thought, though she could think of many things more beautiful than a lump of metal. But she was going to be encased in this metal for over two hours with the man beside her. Close to, his aura seemed to reach over and absorb her own. The subtle aroma of his aftershave appeared headier in the confined space. It combined with the tang of leather from the seats to give an almost animal scent to the interior.

'Do you mind if I open my window a fraction, Signor Mazzoni?' she asked. On the return journey, she must remember to spray herself liberally with her own perfume. He looked surprised, but pressed a button and the window slid open.

'Thanks,' she said, breathing in the familiar carbon monoxide.

'You must call me Francesco,' he stated, shattering any relief she felt.

Kate turned away. She couldn't believe this. Not from him. She'd travelled to meetings with businessmen before and, in her experience, there were two kinds. Those who used the time to catch up on their correspondence or phone calls, and who noticed her presence as much as they would a fax machine. And the others who were programmed to try it on with any female under the age of ninety. Kate had grown accustomed to dealing with the latter fairly tactfully, but never in several lifetimes would she have believed Francesco Mazzoni to be one of them. Hadn't he told her seven years ago exactly what he thought of women like her? Gold-diggers who attached themselves to wealthy men for financial gain?

With that thought uppermost, she turned back to Francesco. 'I would prefer, Signor Mazzoni, to keep this relationship totally professional.'

He stared at her for several moments, like a novice student attempting to understand a difficult language, and then she saw comprehension dawn. Unfortunately he turned away before she could decipher what followed next.

He turned back immediately. 'I should explain . . . ' His face was composed, and only a faint twinkling in the depths of his eyes hinted that he'd been laughing at her. 'Roberto and Elena are close friends. They are very warm, very demonstrative people who will expect you to use their first names. I believe it would instil a jarring note if we insisted on a formal mode of address.'

'Fine.' Kate felt totally stupid. No wonder Francesco had difficulty in hiding his amusement. That a man who'd been linked with beautiful, influential women of all nationalities should bother with a nobody was indeed ludicrous.

'It must be difficult for you.'

Kate glared at him. 'What must?' The

fact that she was a nobody?

He shrugged. 'Working freelance, never being quite certain what your employers are going to be like.'

'Oh, I usually have a pretty good idea.'

'Do you?' Francesco leaned back in his seat and his eyes flickered lazily over her. The effect was like standing too near a blow-torch. She was certain now that there was no amorous intention there, so what was this? Eventually he spoke.

'Antonio Benedetti recommended you to me.'

Caught off-guard, Kate swore. It appeared to amuse rather than offend Francesco.

Of all the people she'd worked for, Antonio had caused the most havoc in the shortest space of time. It had always been a game for him, but the flowers, chocolates and protestations of love had been no joke for her. Her mother beamed every time Interflora delivered another bouquet, her father told her to be careful, and Dominic kept asking what a wedding was.

'I'm sorry if the bloke's a friend of yours, but he should have a government health warning stamped on his head,' she said with feeling.

Francesco laughed. 'You were not aware that our mutual acquaintance is soon to become a model citizen then?'

Kate raised her eyebrows in query.

'His parents have decided to curtail his activities, a bride has been picked, and the nuptials will take place in September.'

'And Antonio is going along with it?' Kate was shocked. Benedetti had an ego as big as a continent. She couldn't imagine anyone telling him what to do.

Francesco gave a low chuckle. 'Oh yes.'

'To an Italian girl?'

'Of course.'

'Of course.' Kate repeated the words and leaned back against the soft leather upholstery. God, how naïve she'd been. Still was. Not once had she ever questioned Nico's assertion that they would marry. She'd been frightened to tell him that she was pregnant, but he was ecstatic. His father wanted grand-children above all things, he'd told her. The old man would give him whatever he wanted now.

Kate sighed. She'd never really know. Ever the master of drama, Nico had wanted to keep it secret until they could travel to Italy and surprise his father. Unfortunately, he'd never got the chance, but Kate had pictured the scene. A palace somewhere in Rome. Enter the younger son, heir to countless millions, with a language student whom he'd met while she was working as a waitress in a restaurant which he frequented. 'This is Caterina!' he declares. 'Her father is a coach driver and her mother is a dinner lady, and this is the woman I have chosen to marry.' Oh yes, Cesare would have been over the moon!

Kate smiled. She'd always thought Nico was so sophisticated, but he'd been barely more than a child himself. Just like her.

A low voice intruded into her thoughts. 'You were a little in love with Antonio perhaps?'

Kate jumped. 'Oh no, not me.' She shook her head.

'I thought you were thinking of him. Your face . . . ' Francesco spread his fingers in an expressive gesture.

'No, I was thinking . . . ' Kate stopped. Was she mad?

A warm smile transformed Francesco's features. 'You were thinking of someone you loved. I feel privileged, Signorina. There is nothing more beautiful than the glow of love on a woman's face.'

His words shook her to the core, both for the sentiment behind them and for the fact that he could read her face so plainly. Unfortunately, she could only respond with sarcasm.

'Strange, I wouldn't have picked you out as a romantic, Signor Mazzoni.'

Her rudeness didn't seem to upset him. His eyes crinkled with amusement

41

as various thoughts flashed through his brain. 'Strange indeed, but there you have it.' He inclined his head towards her in a mock bow, but whether he was being serious or sending himself up, she wasn't certain.

Nor was she certain either why Francesco should choose to be so affable, instead of burying himself in his briefcase and ignoring her. Still, it did mean that she was being conditioned to his presence. She was no longer so likely to arouse his suspicion by overreacting to him.

It did seem a little ludicrous now that she'd lived in fear of this man for seven years. She'd been convinced that if the Mazzonis knew of Dominic's existence, they'd find a way to take him from her.

Kate gazed out at the M1 flashing past. How stupid she'd been to think she represented more than a minor irritation in Francesco Mazzoni's past. He must have forgotten about her the instant he'd stormed out of the tiny cottage in Sussex. The hurt was deep, but she could live with it. It meant that she and Dominic were safe. The Mazzonis might have their fortune, but she had something infinitely more precious.

Francesco was watching her so she gazed back at him levelly. She wouldn't take any risks, but it was wonderful to be rid of this irrational fear. He was just a man — cold, heartless, and unbelievably cruel, but still just a man. Not a demon about to snatch her baby away.

'You have that look again,' he murmured.

'Really?'

Francesco smiled at her. 'Will you tell me about him?'

'No.' *Not a hope in hell, chum*! Even if Nico hadn't been Francesco's brother, she wouldn't have tainted his memory by blabbing about their love to a bored businessman.

'Ah.' A secret smile played on Francesco's lips. She little knew and cared even less what had put it there. Perhaps if she gazed even more pointedly out of the window he would get the message and shut up.

So she did. The sky was a bright clear blue. A perfect summer's day with no storm clouds. No trace of a god poised with a thunderbolt ready to hurl it at the Bentley below.

She was getting a crick in her neck so she sat back. Francesco was waiting. Like all predators, he was simply biding his time.

'Tell me about your son,' he said.

3

A spasm of fear juddered through Kate's body. Why had he waited until now to pounce? What possible reason could he have for pretending not to recognise her?

'How long have you known?' she gasped.

He was staring at her strangely. 'Since yesterday.'

'Then why didn't you say anything until now?' She clenched her fingers to still the trembling.

'I didn't think it was any of my business.'

Kate scanned his face. Something wasn't right. He looked completely bemused by her behaviour.

'Look Kate, I'll admit that I'm old-fashioned.' He spread his palm wide. 'But I don't insist that all female employees with children should wear a wedding ring.'

Blood pounded through Kate's brain. She'd blown it! Her reaction had been totally over the top. Francesco's brow was knotted in suspicion as he attempted to figure out why.

'I do assume you've made adequate arrangements for the boy?' he asked, seconds later.

'Yes, of course I have.'

'Fine. As I said, it's none of my business.' He turned away, propped his elbow on the window ledge and gazed out. Kate sensed the tenseness in his body. He didn't believe her and she couldn't altogether blame him. But what if he decided to take it further and check that Dominic was well looked after while she was at work?

It was hardly likely, was it?

Kate glanced over at him. He was tapping lightly with his knuckles against his top lip. Something was whirring through his mind.

Could she take the chance? Kate gnawed at her fingernail. If only

Dominic hadn't inherited all of Nico's genes. It was her constant joy, but also her constant worry. One glance, even at a photograph, and Francesco would know instantly whose child he was.

'Francesco?' Kate hesitated. She was treading on dangerous ground here, but she had to tell this man something to throw him off the scent.

He turned to her, his face a mask.

'I'm a bit paranoid when it comes to my son.'

He raised an eyebrow as if to convey that that was an understatement.

'His father and I aren't together anymore.' She struggled with the half-truths. 'But his family would like Dominic to live with them.' She took a deep breath. 'I've lived with the fear that they'll take him for years.'

Concern etched over Francesco's features. 'A child should always be with his mother.'

Kate nodded, though she couldn't help wondering whether he would echo the same sentiments if he knew exactly what child they were talking about.

'I swear to you, I've never ever left him unattended,' she said for good measure.

'I believe you, Kate. Forgive me. It was not my intention to pry.' He looked totally perplexed. 'I recalled Mrs Blanchard mentioning that you had a child. I was simply making conversation.'

And then he did open his briefcase and scan through some files, probably considering it a safer option than making conversation with the unhinged individual beside him.

Kate stared unseeing at a magazine for the rest of the journey. What shook her most was the fact that what had just happened had been completely her own fault, and she'd barely scraped out of the situation. Now Francesco thought she was paranoid. That wouldn't normally bother her, but she was beginning to wonder if it was true.

It was a relief when they arrived at the hotel. She could put some space between her and this man, and hopefully he'd forget her strange behaviour.

But as they walked into the foyer, it wasn't only her behaviour that seemed strange. Granted, she expected Francesco to receive star treatment in such a prestigious establishment. She caught sight of the nightly room rate at reception and reckoned that must be what he was paying for. It was the reaction of the other guests to him that astounded her. Or, to be more accurate, the female guests.

The man must be loving all this attention, she decided, as they made their way to the lift amid stares and smiles. She looked up to check that she was right, and looked sharply away again. His face and body were chiselled in granite as he moved stiffly forward, acknowledging no one. It didn't seem to stop women fluttering their eyelashes at him, though a pickaxe would have been a more useful weapon to break through that stony exterior.

He didn't say a word to her from the time they entered the hotel until they paused at her bedroom door. Yep, back to the old arrogant Francesco she knew and hated.

'It doesn't appear likely that Roberto and Elena will arrive much before dinner.' He took out his key card and examined it. 'You are free to spend your time as you wish before then.'

'Francesco?' She regarded him coolly as he turned brusquely away from her.

'Yes?'

'Dinner?'

'Yes?' His brow knitted into a frown.

'What time is it?' Or was she supposed to guess?

'I shall call for you at seven.'

'Fine.' She slid her card into the lock and walked into the room. Without noticing anything about it, she sat on the bed nearest the door and took out her mobile phone. It was switched on and had a signal. Good. Nobody had tried ringing her so Dominic must be

OK. She'd ring him when he got home from school.

Only then did she look about her. Not bad. Kate smiled to herself at the understatement. Mazzoni secretaries evidently travelled in style. She normally found herself stuffed into rooms barely big enough to swing a mouse.

The colour scheme was neutral, broken up with bold prints on the walls and the royal blue fabric of the curtains, twin beds and sofa. A vase of fresh gerberas had been placed on the dressing table and, on the bedside table, sat a bowl of fruit. Kate reached out a hand to test that the impossibly red, shiny apples were real. Determining that they were, she picked up a red delicious and bit into it.

The next thing she had to do was hang up her evening dress in case it creased. Shaking it free of its tissue folds, she surveyed it critically. On the hanger, it looked a little plain, but she had to admit that the assistant knew her stuff when she'd insisted that she try it on. The charcoal silk was so expertly cut that it hugged and flattered even her slight curves. Cut a little lower on the neck than she'd have liked, the bones in the bodice nevertheless contrived to give her a cleavage that she hadn't experienced since she was pregnant. 'Madam looks magnificent!' declared the sales assistant and, even knowing that was mainly commission talk, Kate had grinned back and decided she looked pretty good.

What would Francesco think of it? Kate grimaced as she was caught out in the thought. Why on earth should she wonder that? Who gave a stuff what he thought!

She took another bite of her apple, rammed the wardrobe door closed and went to investigate the bathroom. Oh yes, lots of bottles of samples to play with. She unscrewed a top and sniffed, expecting the usual pine bubble bath fragrance that hotels seemed to buy in by the lorry load. Jasmine, tuberose, and a hint of gardenia escaped instead.

She checked the label and smiled. Designer goodies, no less. If she didn't use them all during her stay, they'd definitely find a home in her suitcase at the end of it.

The bathroom given the seal of approval, Kate turned her attention back to the bedroom. It was an L-shaped room, living and sleeping area at one end and office area at the other. This was novel. Kate surveyed the computer, printer, and other paraphernalia of her trade. Normally she had to tramp the hotel's corridors to use theirs.

And then she saw another door. Ever curious, she speculated what could be behind it. More office equipment? Surely she had everything she needed here? Without another thought, she grasped the handle and opened it.

'Oh!' It wasn't the most original of things to say when you surprise your employer stark naked, but it was all Kate could manage. She slammed the door shut, leaned heavily against it, and closed her eyes. Her mortification was complete when she heard the sound of laughter coming from the other side.

Didn't she have any brain cells left? Why hadn't she been alert to the fact that inter-connecting doors were common in hotels? In her defence, she hadn't come across one before. But that was no excuse! She should have known that if there was all this office equipment on one side, then the boss might want to come back and forth to use some of it.

Curiosity killed the cat. Well, it hadn't actually killed her, more like singed her. That would explain the scorched sensation in her cheeks. She went back into the bedroom and threw the rest of her apple into the waste-paper bin. Somehow, she'd lost all appetite. Then she thrust open the window and stared out over Birmingham.

Inevitably her thoughts turned to the only other man she'd seen naked. Nico had been beautiful, tall and slender, but his body had been that of a youth. As unlike his older brother's as a baby tiger is to a full-grown beast. Much as she hated Francesco, she was forced to give him full marks for physique.

It was as well she was immune to him. And she was immune. The only way she'd touch him with a barge pole would be to shove him in the canal with it.

Kate tried to focus on the city outside. She had to shift this image of naked masculinity out of her brain. Yet, despite all her loathing of the man, she found it impossible. It remained, as solid and provocative as a Michelangelo sculpture in the corner of her consciousness.

'Hell!' Kate cooled her cheek on the glass. Maybe her friends were right — she ought to get out more and get a life. It surely couldn't be normal to react like this.

Idly, she ran her finger through the condensation she'd left on the window, then wiped it hastily away when she saw that she'd written her former lover's name.

Nico. How could she possibly think of another man in a sexual way? It was a betrayal of his memory. She couldn't do it. Not when she'd known perfection in his arms.

With a sigh, Kate turned away from the window. Seconds later, she almost expired when there was a rap at the door. Although she'd never shown any psychic tendencies before, she knew without any shadow of doubt who was on the other side.

Francesco!

Kate's heart thudded. X-rated versions of what he might possibly want scuttled through her brain. What was any man supposed to think when a woman storms uninvited into his room?

Kate bit down hard on her lower lip. How could she have been so stupid? She knew Francesco would never look twice at her in the normal run of things, but he was probably bored. He was a businessman with a free afternoon. The promise of a 'work-out with his secretary had to beat a work-out in the gym, even for him.

A sudden thought occurred to her. The inter-connecting door! As swiftly and as quietly as she could, Kate clicked the lock on it. Now all she had to do was remain quiet and Francesco would believe she'd gone out. Cowardice certainly, but better than the alternative of repelling Francesco's advances. Advances that he had every reason to believe she'd solicited.

'Damn!' Her teeth savaged her lip again as she recalled that Antonio Benedetti had recommended her to Francesco. There had been a glint in his eye when he'd told her. Just what fictions had Antonio regaled him with?

It was quiet outside. Perhaps Francesco had given up.

And perhaps when she looked outside, there'd be a litter of piglets flying past the window!

She should have known that the man was no quitter.

There was another rap, harder this time, and then his voice, low with only a hint of irritation. 'Are you there, Kate?'

Kate expelled the breath she hadn't realised she'd been holding. Her psychic ability was functioning again, and it was telling her that Francesco Mazzoni was fully aware that she was in the room. It was this knowledge that propelled her forward. No longer was she the quivering girl that he'd bullied so mercilessly. She was now a grown woman and would act like one even in his presence. It was unfortunate, but if Francesco was standing outside with any amorous inclination towards her then she was about to disabuse him of it. As she would have already if it had been any other man.

Pausing only to take a deep breath, she swept open the door.

4

'Signor Mazzoni.' The door to her room was open but Kate stood squarely on the threshold.

'Kate,' he said pointedly, though it was said with a smile.

Kate could hardly look at him. Although he was now dressed in a polo shirt and chinos, her brain insisted on relaying the previous uncensored version in glorious Technicolor. As embarrassing moments went, this definitely ranked with the time she'd arrived at the school dance with her dress tucked into her knickers.

'Did you require anything?' His face was inscrutable, his stance non-threatening. For one wild second, Kate wondered what would happen if she said 'yes'.

Sanity prevailed. 'No. I'm sorry. The

59

inter-connecting door ... I didn't realise ...'

He nodded. 'Do lock it from your side. I shan't need to use it.'

'Right.' Had he heard her locking it or was he telling her that she needn't expect any midnight visits? She glanced up to check his expression, but he was already half-way down the corridor.

'Don't let me keep you,' she murmured, and gave the door a swift kick to close it.

For about five minutes, Kate paced around the room. Embarrassment had given way to irritation, but for the life of her she couldn't explain why. It didn't make sense. The last thing she wanted was Francesco Mazzoni's advances, so why should it upset her that he hadn't made any?

No nearer to an answer, Kate decided not to waste the afternoon thinking about it. The next few hours were hers alone. No office or house work, no child to play with. A rare opportunity not to be squandered.

So what should she do?

A quick browse in the hotel brochure decided her. It had to be the swimming pool. She'd brought her costume just in case. Throwing it into a bag along with some shampoo and a towel, she set off for the leisure suite.

The sight of the water caused the usual flutterings of panic, but Kate focused on the changing room door and forced her feet to keep going. It had been two years after Nico's death before she'd gone swimming again. Ironically, it was his son that had made her do it. She was determined that Dominic should be a strong swimmer from the earliest possible age.

As ever, Kate hurried through the changing process. The sooner she was in the water, the sooner her mind would stop dwelling on the past. She adored swimming. The day would eventually come when she would enjoy the pleasure without feeling guilty about it.

Scraping her hair into a ponytail, Kate stood at the edge of the pool.

What a difference from the local baths she took Dominic to! Although there were plenty of people sitting around it, the pool was almost empty. Surely it couldn't be that cold? She wriggled a toe in the water to check and nearly toppled in when she became aware of the person staring at her from the other end.

Damn! Hadn't he said he was playing squash? And why was he still staring at her? There were two bronzed and glamorous females sitting either side of him on the pool edge. Didn't he have enough to look at?

It was probably her costume. Kate compared her navy all-in-one suit with the skimpy bikinis of Francesco's companions. It was definitely due for renewal — she looked as if she were an entrant in the all-schools gala.

Kate curled her toes around the pool edge and prepared to dive. The water was warm. Too warm. She'd endured baths colder than this. But once in the pool, she forgot everything other than the sensation of being there. It had been a long time since she'd experienced the luxury of being able to swim without dodging arms and legs and other people ploughing straight towards her, and she was going to take full advantage of it. Her arms might ache tomorrow but today she was happy. And when she thought her heart was going to explode with the exertion, she flipped over on to her back and allowed herself to go limp. That was probably enough for one day; the blood was pounding through her system like a washing machine on full spin. She waited until it slowed to a delicate wash cycle, and then swam leisurely back to the deep end.

It was a shock to see Francesco still sitting opposite her as she hoisted herself on to the pool side. For thirty glorious minutes she'd forgotten all about him. One of his companions seemed to have disappeared, but the other was still superglued to his side.

Kate was about to leave when he slid

into the pool and started swimming towards her. Despite herself, she felt compelled to watch as he sliced through the water with consummate skill. 'And this is how it's supposed to look,' she murmured, comparing his smooth economic style with her own enthusiastic but less efficient one. She decided to wait until he'd demonstrated his turn, and make her escape while he headed back to his female admirer. Instead, he came to a halt beside her and rested his elbows on the pool ledge.

'You looked as though you were enjoying yourself.' He grinned up at her.

'I was.'

'You are an excellent swimmer.'

Kate skimmed her toes through the water. Was this where she was supposed to compliment him on his own performance? Well, sorry, he might indeed have the body and skill of an Olympic athlete, but she wasn't going to inflate his ego any further by telling him so. 'Do you think so?' she asked instead.

He gave a deep chuckle. 'You know so,' he said, leaving her with the embarrassment of being the one fishing for compliments.

'Would you care for a race?'

Kate stared at him. Was he serious? He must know that the only chance she had of beating him was if she tied his ankles to the handrail of the steps first. Or was that it? She splashed her feet down and covered them both with a spray of water. 'Isn't that just like a man!'

He passed an arm over his face to wipe away the spray. 'What is?'

'Waiting until your opponent is exhausted before challenging her to a race, just so you can beat her.'

Francesco looked bemused for a second and then started to laugh. It was such a ringing, good-humoured laugh that Kate felt momentarily ashamed of the ill-temper which had inspired it. Before he recovered, she crouched on the edge of the pool. 'Three lengths, that's all I can manage,' she said, and dived in.

Despite swimming at her personal best, and the fact that he hadn't been able to dive in, Kate felt Francesco draw level with her just before she turned into the second length. If he'd wanted to, he could have touched the side before her, and this knowledge sapped her final reserves. She'd wanted to beat him on just one length and she'd given it her all. She was determined to swim a second length but knew she had no hope of a third. It was all she could do to drag her exhausted body back to the other side. Her arms felt like iron bars and her legs like concrete bollards.

Clinging to the ledge and gasping for breath, Kate couldn't look at Francesco. He must be laughing his trunks off! How childish was she? She was twenty-six years old, yet her six-year-old son demonstrated more mature behaviour. Why couldn't she just face facts? She was no match for this man. In any department!

'Forgive me. I wouldn't have suggested a race if I'd known you were so tired.' The fingertips touching her shoulder seared into Kate's flesh, but galvanised her into action.

'Sorry, I'm shattered.' She brushed them away as she reached for the handrail and hauled herself up the steps. How she was looking forward to a shower! It was gloriously fierce and she luxuriated in the warm pummelling it gave her body. Hopefully it would stop her feeling so stiff later on. She took her time washing and drying her hair, and felt her natural energy return as she re-applied her make-up. There were still a few hours left before dinner; perhaps she'd have a walk around Birmingham.

'Kate!' She came to a halt a few seconds before he saw her, hoping in vain that the mood he was in would transport him past her unseeing.

'Francesco.' She watched the storm

clouds recede slightly from his brow.

'Afternoon tea?' It was phrased as a question but was in fact a command.

Kate sighed. She wanted to ring Dominic. What had happened to 'you are free to do as you wish until dinner'? She glanced up at him wondering how a polite refusal would be received. The dark clouds had regrouped and there was definitely a chance of thunder. 'Afternoon tea would be lovely,' she said.

Without a word, he turned on his heel and marched back the way he'd come. Kate's stomach grumbled and she realised she was ravenous. Yes, afternoon tea would be lovely, though not with him.

A waiter was clearing the table that Francesco decided to sit at. Wasn't that just typical? Didn't he have enough empty tables to choose from? Kate shot the boy a sympathetic smile.

'I . . . I'm sorry, sir . . . madam.' The waiter coloured with embarrassment as he glanced from Francesco to her. 'I thought you'd finished.'

'Please set another place for the lady.' Francesco retrieved a newspaper from the waiter's tray, shook it out, then disappeared behind it.

Kate empathised with the boy and shrugged her shoulders slightly to convey that even though her companion might be the customer from hell, she was really quite nice. Apart from anything else, she didn't fancy him spitting in her tea.

The assortment of sandwiches and pastries were divine and Kate helped herself liberally. She knew that she ought to limit herself because of dinner that night, but she could never resist cream cakes.

Francesco nibbled on a few sandwiches but didn't seem that hungry. He was engrossed in the *Financial Times* and appeared to have forgotten her existence. She finished her tea, played peek-a-boo with the baby on the next table, then glanced around to see if there were any spare newspapers. There weren't, and she was bored. She glanced at her watch, imagining what Dominic would be doing. He'd be curled on the mat with Penny watching Children's BBC. His Gran would have given him a glass of milk and some biscuits and, when she wasn't looking, he'd be teasing the dog with them.

Kate glanced over at Francesco. Lord, he was only half-way through the paper! Is that what it took to be a tycoon — you had to analyse every column inch?

Why exactly did he want her there? He might as well have borrowed a dummy from one of the display cabinets for all the difference it made. She guessed it had something to do with his two admirers from the pool. They'd glared at her when she'd come in and swept out of the room immediately after.

Kate sighed. Perhaps he intended to make them jealous, but all she knew for definite was that she'd been used. Apart from that, she had no wish to dwell on the games Francesco played with his women.

'You are bored.'

Kate jumped. She was in the process of shredding her napkin on to her plate and hadn't realised she was doing it. She felt like a naughty child as he stared at the pieces with disapproval, and the muscles of her mouth twitched as she held in the laugh that was desperate to escape.

He gazed at her speculatively. 'It is a rare occurrence, I suppose . . . '

'Mmm.' She couldn't remember the last time she'd been bored. She never had the time.

He continued, ' . . . for a beautiful woman like yourself to be ignored in such a fashion.'

She glared at him. Beautiful woman? Was he sending her up?

He folded his newspaper. 'I forget my manners. What shall we discuss?'

Kate gave her napkin another tug. Why did they have to discuss anything? Why couldn't he just tell her to go so he could read his newspaper in peace?

'Oh, I don't know.' She pointed to the *Financial Times*. 'How are your investments doing?' It was a throwaway remark, not consciously designed to irritate, yet apparently it had.

'They are fine,' he grated back.

'That good, eh?' she murmured, waiting for her marching orders.

They didn't come. Instead, his dark eyes scanned her face as though committing it to memory. Disturbed by his look and the silence between them, Kate scoured her brain for something to say. 'Why is this meeting so important?'

'It is my mother's company.' Unwittingly, he provided the piece of jigsaw that had eluded her.

'Elizabeth Webster!' she said triumphantly.

'You know my mother?'

'Er, no,' she said, belatedly realising how her overly-enthusiastic response must have sounded as his eyes narrowed in suspicion.

'Please explain.' He sat back in his chair and crossed his arms.

'I thought I already had.' Francesco's demeanour chilled her. If he ever became tired of being a businessman, the CID would snap him up.

'Remind me.'

'I told you that I always check companies out, so I knew that Tamworth Textiles was owned by Elizabeth Webster. I didn't realise that she was your mother.'

'I see.' Kate saw his body relax, and her mind went off at a tangent. Why was Nico's mother using what she presumed was her maiden name? Had she and Cesare finally divorced? Unfortunately they weren't questions that she could ask Francesco.

'Does your mother own any other companies?' She had to ensure that she never became entangled in such a mess again.

He started to laugh. 'No. One is more than enough.'

'How come?'

He deliberated before answering. 'My mother is English,' he stated, as though that answered a great deal.

'Yes?' She already knew that much.

'A brilliant artist, a brilliant designer. She designs all the textiles for the company.' He smiled at her, and she was touched by his evident pride. Even a rotten apple had some edible bits.

'But her business sense . . . ' He shrugged his shoulders in an expressive Latin gesture. 'When she told me what her year-end profits were, I had to see the books. The company should have made double that. The reason was as I suspected, but I shan't go into details. Suffice it to say that I am now sorting out the problem.'

A question formed in Kate's brain. She knew that it really should stay there, but she had to ask it. 'Doesn't your mother mind you meddling in her affairs?'

For a second, Francesco looked as though she'd punched him. He opened his mouth to reply, but thought better

74

of it and stared at her instead. Then he developed a consuming interest in his teacup. He picked it up and appeared to study the pattern. Finally, he replaced it in the saucer. 'I don't meddle, I help,' he said quietly.

'Right.' Kate knew to drop the subject. She'd scored a point and she was happy. So had he had enough of her conversation now? Could she go?

Apparently not. The waiter had seen him playing with his cup and came to enquire whether 'Sir' wanted a fresh pot of tea. To her surprise, 'Sir' said that he did.

Silence lengthened between them. Francesco sipped his tea and showed no inclination to finish it quickly. He seemed relaxed, but Kate knew that he was playing games with her. The only words he'd said had been in answer to her questions, and she wondered if he'd sit there until five-to-seven if she remained silent.

Finally, she cracked. 'Why did you come looking for me when you'd already started your tea?'

'I didn't come looking for you.' He offered her the fresh strawberry tart that she'd been eyeing for the past twenty minutes.

'No, I'll burst.'

He smiled and replaced it on the table. Kate decided if he didn't continue this conversation, she'd be tempted to pick it up and throw it at him.

'I didn't come looking for you. You happened to be there when I needed you. The perfect secretary.'

Patronising pig! Kate fumed silently.

'That last remark was a joke by the way.' Francesco stared at her strangely. 'You wear your emotions very close to the surface, Miss Thompson. Has anyone ever told you that you don't conceal them very well?'

Kate stared at a chocolate stain she'd made on the white linen tablecloth. What could she say? Certainly not the truth: *I hate your guts, but I thought that I was hiding it pretty well.*

As the seconds ticked by, she decided that her best course of action was to ignore his last remarks. 'So why did you need me?' she asked, as though he hadn't spoken.

He raised his eyebrows at her change of tack, but thankfully declined to comment. 'A beautiful woman is always useful.'

'Oh, why's that?' If he was trying to bait her with the use of the word beautiful, then she wasn't going to rise to it.

He sighed and swept a hand through his hair. 'They follow me everywhere. I try to be polite but sometimes it is difficult.'

'Who are you talking about?' she asked, though she had a fair idea. This was interesting. Did he really not like all the attention he received from women? She found it hard to believe.

'Gold-diggers!' The words punched through the space between them and knocked the air from her lungs. In her mind, she heard him shouting the same words at her, and she closed her eyes in a futile attempt to block the pain. Caught up in his own inner drama, Francesco didn't appear to notice. When she again opened them, he was still ranting.

'Sometimes it feels as though I have my current monetary worth tattooed on my forehead. That is all they are concerned with. Not me as a person.' He came to an abrupt halt and looked across at her. 'Tell me, Kate, can you think of a solution?'

'Yes,' she said, and dug her finger-nails deep into the palm of her hands.

He stilled. 'I would like to hear it.'

'Give it all to charity. That would soon stop them.'

Anger blazed over his countenance and he scrambled to his feet. Then mindful that he was in a public place and was being observed, he sat down again.

Kate's anger had ebbed slightly, and her heart began to pound as she wondered what he would do now. His hands were clenched into fists and he stared at them as he spoke. 'Go now, Miss Thompson.' His voice was low and she had to admire his control. 'I apologise for boring you.'

Kate hesitated, appalled by her rudeness. As a joking remark, she might just have got away with it, but not the way she'd said it. Not with the venom that had infused her voice.

'I'm sorry. That was totally out of order,' she said quietly.

He raised his head and his eyes burned into hers. An apology wasn't enough, she realised. He was waiting for an explanation.

'I suppose you touched a nerve,' she murmured. 'There's you worrying about having too much money, and there's me worrying about having too little.' As he seemed to view the world through mercenary terms, that explanation should suffice. Besides, there was more than a grain of truth in it. She had zero sympathy for his poor-little-rich-boy stance.

'I must apologise also,' he said, taking her by surprise. 'You are paid to act as my secretary, not to listen to my personal problems.'

Oh yes, an apology that put her firmly in her place. Not a surprise at all.

'So if that's all?' she asked, rising to her feet.

With a wave of his hand, he dismissed her.

Two days, she reminded herself.

But she wasn't even half-way through the first one yet!

5

It was five-to-seven before Kate managed to speak to Dominic.

When she hadn't phoned earlier, her mother had decided to take him to McDonald's for a treat. 'What did you have?' she was asking, as there was a sharp rap at the door.

'Just a second, darling.' She raced over to open it, then raced back to the window where there was a better signal.

'A Happy Meal? Lovely. And what kind of toy did you get?' She glanced over at the open door. Francesco had not yet entered. OK, she got the point he was making, but this was the only chance she had to talk to Dominic tonight.

'That sounds great.' She looked up as Francesco entered the room. His look was as dark as the dinner jacket he was wearing. Did he think she'd done this on purpose? That she'd chosen to wait until almost seven o'clock to make a few phone calls?

He remained standing by the door and looked pointedly at his watch. Yep, that was what he thought.

'I won't be able to talk much longer, Dominic,' she said for Francesco's benefit. 'The car? It was a Bentley.' She started to laugh. 'Yes, I suppose it is the best job in the world driving around in one of those.' Again she hazarded a glance at Francesco. To her amazement he gestured for her to continue, then sat down on the sofa.

She turned back to the window. 'No, I'm sorry, love, I haven't a clue what kind of engine the car had. It was a green one though.' From behind her, she thought she heard a snort of amusement, but when she swept around he was looking the other way.

'Oh gosh, I don't know . . . ' Trust her son to want a model of it. 'Tell you what, if gran and grandpa tell me that you've been a really good boy, when I get home we'll go to Hamley's and see if they've got one.' She lifted the receiver slightly away from her ear to drown the yell of glee.

'I have to go now, Dominic. I'll ring you tomorrow. Big kiss. I love you.' She closed her eyes as a surge of longing swept over her. It would pass, she knew, but at that moment she would have given everything she had to be able to cuddle her son.

She turned back to Francesco. 'Sorry about that,' she began but he put up a hand to stop her.

'Don't apologise. There is nothing more important to a young child than a mother's love.' He gave her a broad smile, and for once she returned it.

He remained looking at her. 'You look wonderful,' he said, and gestured expansively with his hands.

Not expecting him to comment at all on what she was wearing, the compliment threw her. 'You don't look so bad yourself,' she said. Even she had to acknowledge that his fan club would be drooling tonight.

He gave her an amused look, then stood up and offered her his arm. Oh God — did she have to?

Yes, it seemed that she did.

She picked up her bag and slid her arm through his. The action seemed profoundly sexual. The silken material of his jacket caressed the fine, downy hairs of her arm and her heart beat faster. Francesco's body heat penetrated the whole length of her figure where it touched his, and it felt as though she was on fire. Combined fragrances of shampoo, shower gel and cologne combined to make her head spin. This was ridiculous! Why was everything so exaggerated with this man?

The walk to the lounge where they were to meet Roberto and Elena seemed to last forever. 'Ah, there they are.' Francesco pushed open the door to a room filled with comfortable armchairs and sofas and decorated in an English country-house style.

On cue, a large bear of a man in his late fifties heaved himself from a sofa and came beaming towards them. 'Francesco, it has been too long.' The two men embraced, and Kate gave Roberto a polite smile over Francesco's shoulder. It was immediately returned, and Kate looked over to gauge whether his wife promised to be so amiable.

Perhaps that had been too much to hope for. Elena was gazing at her stonily and, when Kate smiled at her, she simply looked away.

'You lucky dog!' she heard in a thick Roman dialect beside her, and saw Roberto punch Francesco playfully on the arm. 'Snap this one up quickly, my boy, before someone beats you to it.'

Kate had to turn away to hide her amusement, though she'd have dearly loved to witness the horror on Francesco's face at such words. As she expected, he lost no time in disillusioning Roberto.

'Roberto, may I introduce you to

Kate. She is kindly doing me the favour of acting as my secretary while Teresa is ill. She speaks Italian perfectly.'

As Francesco introduced Roberto to her, the elder man bowed penitently. 'Forgive me, Kate, I meant no offence. I was simply overwhelmed by your beauty.' He took her hand and kissed it extravagantly. 'I am delighted to make your acquaintance, Signorina.'

'And I yours, Signor. No offence taken.' Kate grinned at him. He was completely over the top, but she liked him instantly.

'Charming, totally charming.' He retained her hand in his. 'Come and meet Elena.'

Walking towards his wife, Kate decided that if she had the choice, she'd really rather not. Elena seemed to look even more stony-faced than she had before. She stood up as they approached and, as Francesco effected the introductions, kissed the air on either side of Kate's cheeks. Kate resisted the urge to heat them with her hands afterwards.

So this was Francesco's idea of a very warm, very demonstrative human being? Enough said.

'Why did you not tell us that Teresa had been taken into hospital?' Elena demanded. 'We would have sent flowers. Do you have the address?'

As Francesco dutifully extracted a pen from his pocket, Kate observed the woman and wondered what she might have done to upset her. Elena was dressed flamboyantly in an off-the-shoulder chiffon creation. A stylist must have told her at some time that she needed to wear colour. Unfortunately, they'd forgotten to tell her that she didn't have to wear it all at once.

Kate gave herself a mental shake; she didn't normally have such bitchy thoughts.

'Poor Teresa! Such a horrible thing to happen to such a lovely person!' exclaimed Elena, and Francesco was directed to give details of his secretary's operation.

Kate took a swift gulp of the chilled wine that she'd requested, then tried to pretend that she hadn't as everybody else seemed to have waited until they could raise their glasses in a toast to absent secretaries.

'And so efficient also. This must be causing you tremendous problems, Francesco.' Elena looked pointedly at Kate, who smiled sweetly back. This was a job, she reminded herself. She was being paid extremely well to stand here and take these veiled insults and not retaliate.

Francesco murmured something about someone in the Milan company who could be with him by Monday.

'Not Luisa Condotti?'

Francesco nodded.

'An extremely capable girl.' Elena smiled her approval. 'I know her mother very well. Charming family.'

'I'm sure Francesco will be just fine in the meantime.' Roberto laid an arm along Kate's shoulder.

Elena gave him a look that could

have frozen fire, and he immediately removed it.

Oh Lord, was *that* the reason why Elena was behaving strangely? Did the older woman think that Kate was after her man?

Kate looked across at Francesco. This isn't my fault, her expression told him. I know this is important, and I'm doing my best.

To her surprise, he gave her a wry smile before turning to Elena. 'Don't worry about me, Elena. Kate comes highly recommended.' He offered her his arm. 'Shall we go through to dinner?'

Kate slipped her arm through Roberto's, and they followed the other two. She wondered if Elena objected to her having this physical contact with her husband, but the other woman seemed quite content at the moment, enjoying Francesco's attention and laughing at something he was telling her.

As they walked, Roberto trailed his finger along the dado rail, then examined it. 'Dust!' He came to an abrupt halt and looked at her as though she was responsible.

'Oh?' The inane remark was better than the alternative that popped into her head — which was that he should come round to her house and have a field day!

'And don't you think the paintwork is looking rather tired?'

Kate glanced at the skirting board that Roberto was staring at intently. It looked fine to her. If that was tired, then her paintwork was positively exhausted. 'Maybe it's past its bedtime,' she said, hoping to lighten the situation.

There was a rumble like thunder. It was Roberto laughing. 'You're right,' he said, 'I should learn to cut off from my work.'

Kate frowned. She'd assumed Roberto to be involved in the textile trade, but this didn't seem to be the case. Cleaning? Painting and decorating? It didn't seem to fit.

They arrived at the dining room and

Kate had no further time for reflection. 'Gracious!' she said, as the glare from a dozen chandeliers reflected in ornately gilded mirrors dazzled her.

He came to an abrupt halt. 'What?'

'Oh, er, nothing.' She smiled at him.

'Do tell me. I am curious.'

It seemed that he wasn't going to move unless she told him something, so she told him the truth. 'It's a bit ostentatious, don't you think?' She waved her hand to encompass the heavy gilt chairs, the elaborate floral decorations, and the tables groaning with silver.

Again there was the rumble of thunder. Kate was completely at a loss as to why he should find her personal opinion so amusing. She was even more at a loss when he turned his back to the couple already seated at the table, and pressed his finger to his lips. 'Not a word,' he said. 'This is Elena's taste, not mine.'

'OK.' Kate nodded. 'What kind of hotels do you like?'

This question seemed to cause even more amusement.

'We should sit down.' Kate glanced nervously over to the table. The last thing she wanted was to fuel Elena's suspicion that she was after her husband.

Roberto grinned broadly. 'Francesco didn't tell you, did he?'

Kate shrugged. Whatever Roberto was referring to, she decided that Francesco probably hadn't.

'I own this hotel, Kate,' said Roberto quietly, and enlightenment crashed into her brain like a falling meteor.

'I'm really sorry.' She'd spent too long with Francesco. Now she, too, had developed the skill of being able to insult someone without trying.

'Don't worry about it.' Roberto winked at her and mimed the action of a zip along his lips before leading her to the table.

'At last,' muttered his wife. She regarded Kate coolly. 'You're very thin, my dear. I do hope you're not going to be one of those girls that picks at her food.'

Kate shook out her napkin. 'Not usually.' She wished heartily that she hadn't eaten so much a few hours before; she could have challenged Elena to a competition. In the event, the food was so good that she could have won anyway. This prompted a discussion by Elena on metabolism, and how it was so unfair that some people could over-eat and not put on an ounce, yet people like her had only to look at a profiterole to put on pounds.

Kate drained her glass of champagne to stop herself reminding Elena that she'd only beaten her by an after-dinner mint, put the glass down, then agreed with her completely. She seemed to be gaining plenty of brownie points with Francesco, who smiled encouragement as Elena commented on everything from her hairstyle to the shade of lipstick she was wearing.

As they retired to the lounge for liqueurs, Kate felt decidedly mellow.

She did a quick tally of her alcohol consumption and decided to order a coffee instead. Having her pass out on the sofa might make Elena's millennium, but she didn't think Francesco would be too impressed!

The alcohol had anaesthetised her wonderfully against Elena's remarks however. The woman could criticise all she liked and Kate would just agree with her. On balance, the evening had to be counted a success. Both Francesco and Roberto looked relaxed and convivial. Congratulating herself that they were now on the last lap and that she hadn't fouled up, Kate flopped on to a sofa.

To her surprise, Elena sat down beside her and the two men sat a little way away. Was this where the gentlemen talked business and the women had to keep out of the way? Kate straightened up; there was still work to be done. She smiled brightly at Elena. 'I've been admiring your necklace all evening. It's lovely.' She pointed to the diamond snuggling in Elena's bosom.

Elena sipped at her brandy and gave her the first genuine smile of the evening. Perhaps alcohol had finally thawed her a little. 'Roberto gave it to me. For our silver wedding anniversary.'

And though Kate privately wondered if he'd received a medal in return, what she actually said was, 'Gosh, twenty-five years! You must have been so young when you married.'

'Eighteen.' Elena traced her finger round the rim of her glass and smiled a secret smile. 'My parents were against the marriage. They said Roberto would never amount to anything.'

'But they were wrong,' Kate prompted.

'I always knew they were.' Elena tipped her head back, drained her glass and then signalled to the waiter for a refill. 'Roberto was who I wanted, and Roberto was who I got.'

Kate gave a snort of amusement. She might not like the woman but she had to admire her. She'd obviously been able to spot a winner.

Elena regarded her coolly. 'And have you never behaved thus?'

Kate was about to deny it, when she recalled how she'd traded all her tips with the other waitress on her shift in exchange for being the one to serve Nico. She felt herself colouring. 'Yes, I suppose I have,' she admitted.

It was Elena's turn for amusement. 'You are stronger than you look, Kate. I think I'm beginning to like you.'

Kate thought it was more a case of Elena beginning to get drunk than anything else, but she smiled back. If Elena wasn't so antagonistic towards her, it would make things a lot easier. 'Your parents came around to your point of view in the end?' she asked.

Elena swilled the golden liquid around her glass and chuckled softly. 'Let's just say that we forced their hand a little.'

'Oh?' Kate thought she caught her meaning, but decided to act puzzled. She didn't want to risk upsetting her new friend by jumping to conclusions.

'Don't pretend to be so naïve, Kate,' she snapped. 'It doesn't suit you.'

She was right then. 'How many children do you have?' she asked.

The older woman looked smug. 'Nine.'

'Gosh!' Kate tried to imagine coping with nine Dominics and failed completely. She raised her palms in defeat. 'I'm all admiration. What ages are they?'

For the next half hour, Elena discoursed freely about her family. If only Kate had realised sooner what her favourite subject would be, she might have prevented their earlier friction.

'And what about you, Kate? Have I not convinced you of the joys of motherhood?' Elena looked at her slyly.

'Oh, I already knew that.'

'What, don't tell me that you have children also?'

Kate smiled. 'Just the one.'

'A baby?'

Kate shook her head. 'No. A little boy. Six.'

'Listen to me, Roberto! Can you believe this?' Kate jumped as Elena shouted across to her husband. 'Kate here has a six year-old son!'

Kate bit her lip as everyone turned to stare at her and she caught Francesco's amused look.

'Congratulations, *bella!*' Roberto roared back. 'What is his name?'

'Dominic.'

'Excellent!' Roberto raised his glass.

'We cannot wait for grandchildren,' confided Elena, 'but none of them seem in any hurry to oblige us.' She sighed, then looked pointedly at Kate's ringless fingers. 'These modern couples. I suppose that describes you — living together without the blessing of the church.'

Kate shook her head. 'No. Not me.'

'You have no ring.' Elena stated the obvious.

'No.' Kate felt a lump rise to her

throat. 'Dominic's father isn't around any more.'

'The bastard!' spat Elena. 'And a lovely girl like you. I hope he's still giving you money for Dominic's support?'

'No, he's . . . ' Kate tried to explain but Elena was too quick for her.

'Give me his details.' She withdrew a notebook from her bag. 'Wherever he's hiding, Roberto will be able to find him.'

Kate's head started to spin. 'You don't understand. Dominic's father is dead.'

'Ah!' The older woman gave a cry of pain and swept Kate into her arms. 'You are a widow! You poor child!'

Kate felt totally stupid. Her mother wasn't the hugging type and she wasn't used to such shows of affection. 'We didn't have time to get married,' she murmured.

'Even worse.' Elena's grip on her tightened and she felt herself being rocked rhythmically. She wished she wouldn't. She'd had too much to drink to be jigged about like this.

'And so young,' Elena crooned, patting her on the back.

Kate's head swum. What on earth was Francesco making of all this? Was it really how he expected his secretary to conduct herself? But what was she to do? If she were to pull abruptly away from Elena, she'd only succeed in offending her.

She became emotional. How much of it was the alcohol zipping through her veins and how much was a fellow woman's sympathy melting her defences, she couldn't say. But gathered against Elena's bosom and feeling her comfort flowing into her, Kate had to bite back the tears. Her grief had always been an intensely private affair. Not once had she broken down in front of her parents. She certainly wasn't going to do so here.

Elena stroked her hair. 'How did he die, *cara*?' she asked.

Kate's thoughts pitched back in time.

She hadn't wanted Nico to go swimming, but Nico had always done exactly what he wanted and had gone anyway. Oh Lord, if only she'd been more forceful in those days and had stopped him. 'I . . . It was an accident,' she stuttered. And then the full horror of that accident, of Nico fighting in vain for his life, hit her, and she broke down. She clung to Elena and soaked her with her tears. For several minutes, she let everything flood out.

Without any thought to the consequences.

6

Kate hazarded a glance at Francesco, who was now sitting opposite her. There were only the two of them. 'What on earth have you been saying to the girl to upset her so?' Roberto had demanded of Elena and dragged her away.

Francesco didn't look too angry, though it was difficult to tell. He was stirring a coffee and gazing into its depths, as though hoping to find an answer to the mystery of life lurking there.

Before her, three drinks had been placed — a glass of water, a glass of brandy and a cup of coffee. It reminded her of the fairy tales she'd read as a child. What would happen if she chose the wrong one?

'Francesco?' she whispered, deciding that his reaction would decide the drink she chose.

'Hmm?' His head jerked up, but it was a few seconds before he focused on her. Whatever it was that had absorbed him, it hadn't been her behaviour.

'I'm sorry.' She hesitated. 'What can I say?'

He reached over and touched her hand lightly. 'You don't have to say anything, Kate. It is all right.'

'I managed to ruin the evening.'

'You ruined nothing.'

Kate spooned sugar into her coffee. 'You're just being nice,' she said.

This seemed to amuse him. 'This has been a day of surprises,' he chuckled. 'I never thought I'd hear you call me nice.'

Kate concentrated on her coffee. She knew exactly what he meant.

'Perhaps this isn't the best time to ask,' he said softly, 'but it is puzzling me . . . ' He waited until her eyes met his, until he was able to probe their depths.

'What?' Her grip tightened on the coffee cup.

'I wondered if perhaps we'd met before?' he asked, and it was a wonder that the cup didn't shatter into a thousand pieces.

'My business interests are wide,' he continued. 'There are times when I have bought a company, and then been forced to make some of the workforce redundant in order for that company to survive. Have you or your family been involved in something like that?'

She forced her fingers to relax their hold on the cup, and shook her head. 'No.'

He pursed his lips in exasperation. 'Kate, I can't defend myself if I don't know what the charge is.'

'There isn't any charge,' she lied. 'You've spent too long with me. If you're not careful, you'll end up as paranoid as I am.'

He clicked his tongue in disgust and turned away. Evidently she'd failed to convince him.

'Would you let me have Elena and Roberto's phone number in the hotel?' she asked, changing the subject.

He raised an eyebrow in query.

'I'd like to ring them to apologise. Elena was kind. I can't bear the thought of Roberto blaming her for what happened.'

'I'm sure Elena will already have corrected Roberto on that point.' Francesco checked his watch. 'Besides it's too late now.'

'Surely they won't be asleep yet?' persisted Kate, then realised from his look of amusement how ridiculous she sounded.

'Asleep? No.' He watched her face, knowing that the images scuttling through her brain were the same as in his.

Disturbed by his scrutiny and wanting it to stop, she blurted out the first thing that entered her head. 'They've been married twenty-five years,' she said and he could contain his amusement no longer.

Kate could only grin back. If their positions had been reversed she'd have reacted exactly the same. 'I've been reading too many *Postman Pat* bedtime stories. Mr and Mrs Goggins certainly don't get up to stuff like that,' she said, and he laughed harder.

As she watched him, Kate felt a stirring deep within her. She tried to tell herself she'd eaten too much and that it was indigestion, but she knew that it was a lie. In a good humour and with no hint to the darker side of his nature, Francesco Mazzoni was an extremely attractive man. If she could react like this, what hope was there for the rest of womankind?

He relaxed into a companionable silence and she was left to her reverie. It must be so easy for the man. Any other secretary, having been wined and dined and subjected to his charm, would probably be all of a flutter by now and wondering if she was going to receive an invitation to his lair. She wondered what his permanent secretary was like, and then she stopped wondering about anything.

The hand on her shoulder startled her.

'Bed,' he said, smiling.

'What?' She jerked away as though he'd branded her. 'No. No way!'

Two streaks of red flashed across his cheekbones. 'Whatever you wish, Kate,' he ground out. 'It was merely a suggestion, not an order. You'd fallen asleep. I thought you'd be more comfortable upstairs than down here.'

He rammed his hands into his pockets. Unrestrained, they'd probably have reached over and throttled her. 'It is certainly where I intend to go. I'll wish you goodnight.' And with that, he turned on his heel and marched out of the room.

Oh, hell! Well done Kate! Another bout of grovelling coming up. She scrambled to her feet and raced after him. He was standing by the lift, his back so stiff that it was threatening to crack.

She took a deep breath and slipped her arm through his. 'I seem to spend half my life apologising to you,' she said.

'There is no need for apology.'

No. Not much. Kate glanced up at the closed, uncompromising face that wouldn't even look at her. She might have misinterpreted his advances completely, but she'd bet that there weren't that many women who'd rejected them so soundly. Despite it all, satisfaction blossomed inside her. He'd forgotten their first encounter completely, but she'd lay bets that it would be some time before he forgot their second.

'Anyway, I'm sorry. I was asleep. I must have been dreaming.'

'Humph!' he snorted, unconvinced.

She was reminded of Nico. He'd often had bouts of ill humour and had to be coaxed out of them. It struck her that she wouldn't have the patience now, but she had to make an effort with his brother.

'Thanks for a lovely evening,' she

said, and this time he did look at her. Reminded of his assertion that her face displayed her feelings, she flushed.

He gave an almost imperceptible shake of his head then turned his attention to the indicator panel above the lift.

'The food was glorious,' she attempted but, as this was met by zero response, she decided to give up.

'Why was Elena such a bitch at the beginning of the evening?' she asked when the lift doors opened.

Momentarily, his lips twitched, but stilled as he turned a stern face towards her.

'Well she was.' Kate rested against the panelled walls of the lift. This day seemed to have lasted a lifetime.

'Elena was a great beauty,' said Francesco, as though this should explain everything.

Kate shrugged. 'She's not exactly ugly now.'

'I had a suspicion that she might feel threatened by your beauty, but it seemed pointless mentioning it and causing you anxiety beforehand.'

'My beauty?' Kate looked at him to see if he was sending her up. He gazed steadily back and she was unable to tell. 'I'm just ordinary,' she stated, not believing that anyone could feel threatened by her.

He gave a derisive snort. 'You are anything but ordinary, Kate.'

From anyone else, she would have taken this as a compliment, but the angry note in his voice confused her. The lift halted at the fifth floor and they walked the short distance to her room in silence.

'Goodnight, Kate,' he said shortly, and was about to continue to his room when she spoke.

'I am sorry about what happened with Elena, Francesco. I didn't do it on purpose to ruin things.'

His eyebrows shot upwards in surprise. 'It never occurred to me that you had. If anything, I was pleased that you felt so comfortable in Elena's presence that you were able to release your emotions as you did.'

'Oh!' It was her turn to be surprised. That was quite a nice thing to say.

And then he spoiled it.

'Don't worry about it, Kate. It was probably to my advantage rather than the reverse.'

Kate pondered his words. Was that the reason he didn't want her phoning Elena and Roberto? If Roberto thought that his wife had upset her, he'd be more amenable at tomorrow's meeting? She decided that sounded about right.

'Goodnight Francesco,' she said, and slid her key card into the door.

★   ★   ★

Whatever the reason, the meeting the following morning seemed to go better than Francesco expected. He betrayed no emotion during it, but afterwards his satisfaction was almost palpable.

'Excellent work!' His praise apparently included her as she sat with the

111

lawyers in the conference room checking the finer details of the contract
before signature.

To her relief, Roberto had winked
at her when he first entered the
room, before adopting the mask of
the professional businessman for the
remainder of the meeting.

Negotiations had always fascinated
Kate from the time she'd trained as a
secretary. She liked to watch the main
players side-stepping each other and
giving way on one point to gain
another, and she prided herself on
being able to predict the outcome in the
first few minutes.

She watched this meeting with
particular interest, and soon discovered
that it was different from all others
she'd attended. Francesco and Roberto
seemed merely to be going through the
motions of arguing. It puzzled her until
she realised that they must have already
decided everything the previous evening
when she was with Elena. So if that was
the case, why had Francesco been in

such a strange mood when he'd walked her back to her room last night? Surely he should have been elated then?

'A toast.' Francesco handed out glasses of champagne. 'To the success of my mother's business.'

Kate raised her glass. She'd drink to that, but only a sip. Colloquial Italian was easy, but legalese was difficult in any language. She needed a clear head and full concentration to ensure she got it right.

Francesco perched on the edge of her desk. The action of her fingers across the keyboard seemed to fascinate him, but it caused her to stumble over the keys.

She paused for a moment. 'Your mother will be pleased about today,' she said in the search for something to say to him.

'You don't know my mother,' he answered cryptically.

'No.' Elizabeth was the only one of Nico's family that she was disappointed not to have met. When Nico had moved to Sussex with her and refused to work in the family business, Cesare had cut off his allowance. Nico had soon worked his way through Kate's meagre savings and, when it was all gone, had applied to his mother for funds. Though now she would feel uncomfortable at such an arrangement, at the time Kate had only been grateful to Elizabeth because it meant Nico could stay with her.

'So your mother won't be pleased?' she probed.

He gave a distinctly Latin shrug. 'Mama will show her pleasure in her own inimitable fashion, I expect,' he said, which told her nothing at all. Much the same as Nico.

He stood up and walked away, which at least enabled her to return her full attention to her work.

To her surprise, everything was completed by one o'clock. She'd been under the impression that they wouldn't be leaving the hotel until late afternoon and, as she nibbled on the sandwiches Francesco had had brought in to save breaking for lunch, Kate started to feel excited as she planned how she could spend the rest of the day with Dominic. She hadn't allowed herself to dwell on how much she missed him, but now that it was nearly over, she acknowledged that his absence felt like a hole in her heart.

Francesco, too, seemed eager to be away. 'Is there any chance I could have a quick word with Elena before we leave?' she whispered, as the last items were being finalised.

'Elena has gone shopping,' said Francesco, but added as he saw the look of disappointment that crossed her face, 'Don't worry, Kate, you will see her again. Now that you have touched her heart, Elena will forever be inviting you to family occasions.'

'Oh.' This wasn't at all what Kate envisaged. All she had wanted was to thank Elena for her kindness, not to become bosom buddies. Her link with the Mazzoni family made that far too dangerous, especially if the invitation should include Dominic.

'I'll just write her a quick note if you don't mind' she said. She'd have to field any invitations if and when they came.

'Whatever you wish.'

Half an hour later, they were seated in the Bentley. 'You look happy,' Francesco smiled.

'Mmm.' Kate was about to say that she couldn't wait to see Dominic, but changed her mind. She didn't want to encourage any more questions about her son. 'I'm happy to be going home,' she said instead.

From the tightening of the muscles of Francesco's jaw, she realised that her remark had been tactless. Oh hell, she wasn't going to apologise to him again. It was his fault for taking it personally. She rested back against the soft upholstery and because further conversation wasn't forthcoming, closed her eyes. The motion of the car combined with the glass of champagne she'd drunk when everything had concluded was making her sleepy, and a sweet lethargy settled over her limbs.

An hour passed before Kate dragged herself back to the present. She woke, disorientated, and gave a small cry when the profile of Francesco Mazzoni came into focus.

'Hmm? Bad dream?' He gave a languorous stretch and she wondered if he, too, had been asleep. He smiled. 'We're almost there.'

'What?' She couldn't have been asleep that long. She checked her watch, but it must have stopped, so she looked outside to see where they were. Then she dug her fingernails into the tender flesh of her palm to check that she was in fact awake. The resulting pain assured her that she was, but if this was London then she must have dropped into a different dimension while she slept!

They were travelling along a country lane flanked by lush hedgerows. The Bentley had slowed to navigate the twists and turns in the road, and every few minutes there was an ominous scratch as an overhanging branch scraped along the paintwork.

Panic ripped through Kate's system. Surely he couldn't be kidnapping her? No. There had to be a logical explanation. But what on earth could it be?

'Where are we, Francesco?' Her voice shook as she attempted to still her fears.

She jumped as another branch rasped against the window.

'Where the hell are we?' she demanded.

7

Francesco's brow was furrowed as he turned to her. If he didn't like her tone then he'd better explain what was going on. Quick. He scanned her face, then evidently not liking what he read there, tapped his knuckles against the car window. 'We are near Ludlow, in Shropshire,' he answered coldly.

'Ludlow! What the bloody hell are we doing in Ludlow?' Kate could no more contain her language than she could her shock.

'We are going to visit my mother.' Francesco's expression was tight.

'Your mother?' Panic resurfaced, then seeped away as Kate reassured herself that she had nothing to fear from Nico's mother. Elizabeth couldn't identify her. They hadn't even spoken on the telephone. 'Great. Just great,' she mumbled. 'Thanks a bunch for letting me know.'

'You were asleep.' Francesco was having difficulty keeping his temper. She recognised the signals — she felt like lashing out too.

'I do not intend to stay long.' Francesco's voice was as cold as a mortuary slab. 'But don't worry, Kate. If we are not back in London by the allotted time, you will receive overtime.'

Kate glanced at him in disgust, then had to turn away before she told him to stuff his overtime. Wasn't this just like a Mazzoni! Arrogant, uncaring, self-centred and dictatorial. He'd decided on a whim to visit his mother and so they were going. Her life, her family, weren't important. They could be bought with a few extra pounds.

Despite it being a brilliant summer's day, it was growing dark inside the car. The path they were following had become narrower and the trees on either side of the road linked their branches in a dense green canopy shutting out the light. As the car slowed to little more than a walking pace, Kate's stomach churned. Nature didn't seem to want her to get there. She gasped as they came to an abrupt halt.

Beside her, Francesco sighed. 'If I didn't know better, I'd swear that my mother did this to deter visitors.' They both watched as Derek got out of the car to remove a broken branch that was blocking their path. He heaved it to one side and the car continued its slow progress before swinging through a tall stone archway. There didn't appear to be any gates attached to the pillars on either side to dissuade uninvited guests, but with the pathway leading to the entrance in such a condition they were hardly necessary.

Nature had not exactly been tamed on the other side of the archway, but it was no longer so rampantly in command. As they continued along the drive, huge bushes of hardy fuschia replaced the canopy of trees, with flowers ranging from pink to blood red. Fuchsias gave way to roses, which appeared to have been planted with little regard to colour. Pink jostled its orange neighbour, which in turn competed with a vivid scarlet as to which looked the most gaudy. Between them all, seedlings of borage, cornflower, marigold and whatever else had been blown by the wind were allowed to flourish without any fear of uprooting. Kate couldn't help but compare this with her own mother's regimental style of gardening. She'd have a fit if she could see this one.

They came to a standstill before a timber-framed manor house. Kate had no time to comment on its beauty before Francesco was out of the car and waiting for her at the bottom of the steps. When she joined him, he walked up to the heavy oak door and inserted his key into the lock.

Kate was surprised. She had a key to her parents' house, but she wouldn't have dreamed of barging in without knocking to see if they were at home.

The hallway was a shock. It was

painted a vivid pink that was so out of keeping with the exterior and age of the house that Kate caught her breath. She quickly realised that that was its intention — to shock — and she couldn't help but wonder what type of person lived in a house like this?

She didn't have much time to dwell on it as she followed Francesco through a maze of corridors. 'If she's not in here, she'll be in the studio,' he announced, flinging open the door to the kitchen.

A girl of about twenty raised a shaved head from the magazine she was reading and smiled briefly. 'Hi. How you doing? There's some coffee on.' She jerked her head towards a percolator, but made no attempt to get up or to remove her red Doc Marten boots from the pine kitchen table.

'Hello, Rose.' Francesco's face was a mask. She couldn't tell whether he was annoyed by the girl's behaviour or not. So who was she? Nico had never mentioned such a name. Perhaps she was a distant relation.

'Where is my mother?'

Rose turned over a page of her magazine. 'Where she always is.'

'Then please tell her that her son has arrived and would like to see her. We haven't much time so I would be grateful if you could do it today.'

Rose pulled a face in response to the sarcasm and grudgingly got to her feet. She paused before Kate and peered at her. 'I know you, don't I?' she demanded.

Kate shook her head. 'No.' She'd definitely have remembered.

But Kate didn't seem convinced. 'What's yer name?' she demanded.

'Kate.'

'Nope. Don't ring any bells.' The girl shrugged and walked off.

Kate turned to Francesco, who was lifting down mugs from an old pine dresser. She was impressed that, even though he wasn't looking at her, he knew what she wanted.

'One in a long line of waifs and strays

that have been taken in by my mother.' He filled the mugs with coffee. 'She is employed as a domestic help, but spends most of her time making *papier mâche* masks.'

His hand hovered over the sugar bowl. 'One spoon, I believe?'

Kate was surprised that he'd remembered.

'Apparently she has a talent for masks.' He shrugged expressively. 'I suppose we should be grateful that she has a talent for something.'

He handed her a mug as Rose clomped back into the room. 'She won't be a minute. She's just finishing off the cat's paw. She doesn't want the paint to dry up and change colour.' Rose resumed her seat and replaced her feet on the table.

'Cat's paw?' Francesco frowned. 'She didn't mention she was including cats in the designs.'

Rose wrinkled her nose. 'Hate the awful things. They bring me out in a rash, but she promised Mrs Avery.'

'Mrs Avery?' enquired Francesco. Kate had to admire his patience.

'Barmy old woman from the town. She brought this photo of a cat that she'd had for fifteen years. She had to have it put down and she was crying and everything, so Elizabeth promised to paint its portrait. I'd have told her to take a hike, but you know your mother.'

Francesco sighed 'I do indeed.' He handed the girl a mug. 'Would you take this out to Derek please.'

'Yeah. OK.' She put it on the table, bent over, and took a mouthful of the steaming liquid.

'Rose!' Francesco looked appalled.

'You filled it too full. I'd only have spilled it all over the floor if I'd tried to carry it out like that.'

Kate was still grinning when the kitchen door was flung open and the statuesque presence of Elizabeth Mazzoni swept through it. Swept was definitely the word. Although she was at present barefoot and dressed in a paint-spattered smock, this was a woman who was used to grand entrances. Kate watched with interest as she opened her arms wide and gathered her son into an embrace that appeared more theatrical than emotional.

'You look well, Mama,' said Francesco, being the first to pull away and brushing idly at a splodge of red paint that had transferred to his jacket.

'Pillar box red!' exclaimed Elizabeth, delighted. 'You must wear that colour more often. It suits you.'

'I'll be sure to remember that,' said Francesco drily.

'Now what about you?' Elizabeth traced an imaginary shadow under Francesco's eye. 'You are working too hard, I see. Take a break. Have some fun.'

'I am in perfect health, Mama, and perfectly happy.' Francesco took her fingers away from his face and brushed them against his lips. 'And I can't stay long, so we must talk about business. Your business. There is much to discuss — both good and bad.'

'Pah, business.' Elizabeth shook her head disparagingly, causing her long, silver-streaked dark hair to ripple across her back.

'There are more important things in life than business, Francesco.' She smiled at Kate, seeming to notice her for the first time. 'Love, for example. Tell me that you have fallen in love with this delightful child and have brought her here for my approval.'

'Behave yourself, Mama.' Francesco's voice was milder than she would have expected. 'Kate is a temporary replacement for Teresa.' Francesco drew her forward for introduction.

'And a vast improvement also.' With a wide smile, Elizabeth took Kate's hand and squeezed it firmly. 'I'm pleased to meet you, my dear.'

'And I you, Mrs Mazzoni,' she replied, not knowing if she preferred her maiden or married name.

'Call me Eliz . . . ' the older woman began, then faltered. She gripped

Kate's hand and searched her eyes for the secret hidden there. 'Caterina?' she murmured, using the name that Nico had always favoured.

'I beg your pardon?' Kate forced herself to sound puzzled, though she felt the blood drain from her face.

'This is such a shock. Forgive me one moment.' Kate watched with horror as Elizabeth's composure shattered. She staggered towards a kitchen chair and slumped heavily down on it, causing her son to race over to her aid.

'Hey, what's going on?' Rose burst into the room and looked from her white-faced employer to her grim-faced son, and finally to Kate, who could only speculate what she looked like.

'Go away, Rose!' said Elizabeth and Francesco in unison.

'Fine.' Rose's face curled into a scowl. 'I know when I'm not wanted.' The door slammed behind her.

Kate fought the panic that rose in her chest and tried to think clearly. How had Elizabeth connected her with

Caterina? They'd never met, so the only explanation had to be a photograph she was unaware of. If she kept her wits about her, she could get out of this. She had changed so much since then. Her hair no longer hung in long straight strands to her waist and she no longer wore the long skirts and dresses which she'd once favoured.

'Oh, my dear, after all this time.' Elizabeth gazed up at her. 'You did know my son, didn't you?'

'I've only known Francesco for a couple of days,' Kate replied deliberately.

Elizabeth took a deep breath and sighed it down to the soles of her feet. Then, resolute, she stood up. 'Come with me.' It was a command, and Kate had no choice but to obey. Elizabeth strode out of the kitchen and towards the back door of the house. Kate followed more slowly and, behind her, in case she had any thoughts of escape, followed Francesco.

'What the hell is this, Kate?'

demanded Francesco, drawing level with her as they continued over a cobbled walkway towards another building, which Kate assumed by its vast windows was Elizabeth's studio.

'I haven't the foggiest idea.' Kate couldn't look at him. She could hardly hear him either due to the thundering of her heart in her ears. She had to get a grip! She could still bluff her way out of this if she kept her head. So she was going to look a little bit like a girl in a photograph his mother was going to produce. She would agree that, yes, it certainly did look like her but, no, it couldn't possibly be. If she were convincing enough, they'd have to believe her. And Nico would have to forgive her for denying that she'd ever known him. She was doing it for the best of reasons. To protect his son.

'My darling, come and see. It was always meant for you.' Elizabeth took her hand and tugged her into the middle of the studio while she rifled through some canvases.

'Mama!' Francesco's voice was stern, though the hand on his mother's arm, trying to coax her away from the paintings, was gentle.

'Not now, Francesco!' Irritated, Elizabeth pushed him away.

'There. See!' She dragged out a huge canvas and beamed at Kate, who recognised herself as the medieval maiden in the portrait. A garland of ivy formed a coronet around her head, and roses, lilies and daisies were twined through hair that flowed loosely past her waist. Nico stood beside her, a knight in silver armour, brandishing a gleaming sword. The portrait was romantic and sentimental, and would normally have had her laughing her socks off, but she'd never felt less like laughing. As she gazed at the painting and realised exactly how talented Nico's mother was, the room began to spin. The person standing beside Nico was her. There was absolutely no way of denying it.

Elizabeth clapped her hands in glee.

'Nico sent me lots of photographs. He wanted it to be a surprise. For your wedding day!'

It was the last thing Kate heard before she dropped on to the rush matting that covered the studio floor.

8

She came to as she was being carried over the cobbles. For a second, the sensation of being held in Francesco's arms, of being pressed close to his chest, was a pleasurable one. Then her senses returned fully.

'Put me down!' she screamed, struggling to right herself. She succeeded, only to topple against him again as her equilibrium failed to return.

'Take my arm,' he suggested, and for the present she had no alternative but to comply.

'I hate you, Francesco,' she said, as he led her back to the house. 'I hate you so much.' She had nothing to lose now. After all these years, she could finally face him and tell him so.

But the scenario she'd pictured so often in her dreams was wrong. His hand closed over the one holding on to his arm and squeezed it briefly. 'I know,' he said simply.

'So you finally worked it out!' Kate felt her strength return, and pulled away from him. 'Congratulations, Francesco. It took long enough.'

'Kate, I . . . ' he began, but she put her hands over her ears.

'Stop it! I don't want to hear it!' He continued speaking, so she pressed harder until all she could hear was the roar inside her head. Finally his lips stopped moving and she took her hands away. 'Anything you wanted to say to me should have been said a long time ago,' she said before he could begin to speak again.

He held up his palms in defeat. 'Perhaps now is not the best time.'

'Oh darling.' Elizabeth raced out to meet them as they approached the house. 'Do come in. So stupid of me. I shouldn't have startled you with the portrait like that, but I was so pleased to see you. Do say you forgive me?' Her hazel eyes beseeched Kate to say yes.

'Of course I do,' she answered numbly.

'I'm making you a cup of tea, but perhaps you'd like something stronger?'

'Tea's fine.'

Elizabeth waited until Kate was seated on a chaise longue in the main drawing room and had taken a sip of the tea she'd brought before pulling up a chair beside her. 'Francesco mentioned something about a child,' she ventured.

The cup clattered on its saucer as Kate's hand shook. She darted a glance at the person responsible. He was standing by the window, ostensibly gazing out over parkland, but she could see by his rigid stance that he was fully aware of everything that was happening in the room.

'He would,' she said and saw his shoulders stiffen further.

'I never dared hope . . . ' began Elizabeth, but got no further before she began to sob noisily.

Kate could only look on with embarrassment. She knew that some-one like Elena would have gathered Elizabeth into her arms and given her a hug, but she couldn't do it. 'Oh hell' she murmured, until the situation was alleviated by Francesco crouching in front of his mother and drawing her to him.

'Come now, Mama,' he whispered when Elizabeth had stilled. 'You're upsetting our guest.'

Immediately, his mother pulled away. 'You must think me a stupid old woman.' She rubbed violently at her eyes.

Kate shook her head. 'No. I don't think that at all.' She understood the woman's emotion perfectly.

'You had a little boy?'

'Dominic.'

Kate saw the struggle as the woman fought her tears again. 'Because it has Nico's name in his?'

'Yes.'

Elizabeth smiled, her eyes moist with

tears. 'Your son has half my son within him.'

'More than half.' Kate smiled back.

'I don't think I follow.'

'Dominic is the absolute image of his father.'

'Oh.' Elizabeth hugged herself involuntarily. 'Oh Lord.' Then her eyes blazed an impassioned plea. 'Do say you have a photograph with you?'

Kate nodded. 'In my bag.'

Elizabeth turned to Francesco, who'd retaken his stance by the window, but before she could utter a word of command, he'd left the room. He returned a moment later with her handbag, and handed it silently to Kate.

She unzipped the inner pocket and fished out the make-up bag, where paranoia had made her hide the photos of Dominic which she always carried with her. She hesitated before handing them to Elizabeth. 'I did warn you,' she said, knowing that a hundred warnings wouldn't lessen the shock she was going to give Nico's mother.

Elizabeth gave a gasp as she saw the first one, and her body began to shake. 'Oh, my dear,' she said, laying down the last one and turning to Kate, her arms wide. This time, Kate did feel able to hug her and the two women clung to each other in mutual comfort.

Kate became aware of Francesco's presence beside her. She looked up to see him staring fixedly at the pile of photographs. 'May I?' he asked softly.

Kate shrugged, though she was extremely interested to see how he would react to them. If he became emotional, then she'd know that even if he cared for nobody else, he'd cared something for his brother.

She was destined to be disappointed. Francesco picked up the photos, straightened them carefully, and took them out of the room. Whatever emotions the photos triggered would be enacted in private.

'You mustn't blame him too much,' said Elizabeth quietly.

'No.' Kate wasn't going to argue with her. She was his mother. It was her job to be on his side. Then a thought struck her. 'Did he tell you what happened?'

Elizabeth nodded. 'You must remember, darling, that he'd just lost his brother.'

'Oh yes? And just who exactly did he think I'd just lost?' She stopped. This served no purpose. Elizabeth wasn't the person she should be angry with. 'I'm sorry,' she said.

'From what Francesco told me, you have every right to be angry.'

'Mmm.' And she'd bet that Elizabeth didn't know the half of it.

'He tried everything to find you afterwards, but you'd vanished!'

Kate was reminded of Elena's assertion that Roberto could find anyone. So how hard had Francesco tried to find her? She couldn't imagine he'd searched too rigorously but, not wanting to alienate his mother, she decided to change the subject. She told her of Dominic's passion for cars, and when

Francesco returned they were still discussing the Mazzoni male's fascination for four-wheel toys.

'Francesco was exactly the same.' Elizabeth gestured expansively at him as he entered the room.

'Was he?' Kate was more concerned to see what reaction, if any, the photos had wrought.

Nothing, seemed to be the answer. Not one iota of emotion flickered across the impassive face that was gazing back at her. 'Your son is a fine-looking boy.' He handed her the photos.

'Yes, he is.' She snatched them back. He looked surprised, but Elizabeth didn't seem to notice.

'Oh, my darling, we have so much to talk about. Will you stay here tonight? You are very welcome.'

'I'd rather get back, thanks.' Kate smiled her regret.

'Of course, of course, you are missing your son. It is understandable. Then you will come next weekend and bring

Dominic? Do say yes.'

Kate considered the logistics of getting to Elizabeth's remote spot by public transport, accompanied by an energetic six-year-old. It wouldn't be quite the same as a ten-minute bus ride to see her own mother.

'It's the summer holidays in a fortnight,' she offered. 'We could come then. Maybe stay longer if you wanted us to.'

'Excellent!' Elizabeth clapped her hands and looked at Kate expectantly.

'And you're welcome to visit us before then,' she added, as she was expected to.

Elizabeth reached over and hugged her. 'I am so happy!'

'I am sure that my father would also be happy to be granted the same privileges.' The deep voice echoed ominously around the room.

Kate laughed out loud. Happy? Cesare Mazzoni? She could just imagine him in the tiny bedroom of her Hounslow flat. She'd move out of her room and share with Dominic for the duration of Elizabeth's visit, but there'd have to be a bomb in it before she'd move out for Cesare.

Francesco was now standing opposite her.

'There's no way that your dad's getting an invitation to my house,' she said when he didn't speak.

He perched on the edge of an armchair. 'That is not exactly what I meant,' he said mildly. 'I know that my father would be overjoyed if Dominic visited him in Rome.'

'Oh? Too much trouble for him to come over here, is it?'

Francesco sighed at her contrariness. 'What do you want, Kate?'

'I don't want your father ever to meet Dominic!'

He spread out his fingers in a gesture of puzzlement. 'Why?'

'Because Nico hated his father!'

'That is not true.'

'Then why did he say it?'

'Because papa did not indulge him in

143

everything he did.' Perhaps it was her imagination, but this statement seemed directed at Elizabeth, who didn't look up but continued staring at her fingers, twisting the rings on them backwards and forwards.

'You don't hate someone just for that,' she asserted.

'My point exactly.' Francesco paused for emphasis. 'You were living with my brother, Kate. You must have witnessed how upset he became if he was thwarted in any way.'

Kate bit her lip. Yes, she'd seen it, but she wasn't going to admit it to him.

Knowing he had the advantage, Francesco pressed his case. 'He would say he hated anyone who didn't allow him his own way. I expect he even told you that he hated me.'

Kate stared at him. No, he never had. Which surprised her very much.

But it still didn't change anything. 'I don't want to take Dominic to Rome to meet your father,' she insisted. It wasn't what Francesco wanted to hear and his face darkened. Now who was getting upset when he was thwarted?

'As you wish,' he ground out. 'We'll hire the best nannies in the country to take him in your place.'

She swore at him, then looked at Elizabeth. Where was her support? Elizabeth didn't meet her gaze. Apparently she was on her own. 'We're talking about a six-year-old boy here, Francesco,' she began.

'Whom you were quite happy to leave for two days while you accompanied me on a business trip,' he continued smoothly.

'There is a difference.' It was difficult to restrain her impulse to slap him. 'My parents are looking after him. He's known them all his life.'

'Then let them accompany him. They'll be well reimbursed for their trouble.'

'Oh, don't be so stupid,' she said, though she knew Francesco was anything but. His remark about her parents might have been flippant, but it was

145

meant to convey that any reason she might give to keep Dominic and Cesare apart would not be accepted. He was like an Alsatian that had stumbled on a year's supply of doggie treats. They mightn't belong to him but he wasn't going to give them up without a fight, and anybody who tried to take them away was likely to end up savaged.

'What do you think, Elizabeth?' she asked. The woman hadn't struck her as the timid type.

'Dominic is Kate's son,' she answered, not looking at her but at Francesco.

'He is also very much Nico's, Mama. You've seen the photographs.'

'Nico is dead, Francesco. We have no rights in this matter.'

'Rights no, but what about needs? Forgive me, Mama, but you were quick enough to cajole Kate into granting you a visit. How would you have felt if she'd denied you?'

Kate sighed and fished her mobile phone out of her bag. She couldn't imagine them getting back to London any time soon, and she had a desperate need to speak to Dominic. 'I'm going to make a phone call,' she announced, rising to her feet.

'Yes, yes, darling.' Elizabeth gave a general wave in her direction. 'Use any of the phones.'

Ten minutes chatting to Dominic revived her. Not enough to face what was happening in the drawing room, but she pushed open the door anyway. Both Francesco and his mother stopped what they were saying and stared at her. In a lighter mood, she might have given them a twirl or a curtsey, but all she felt now was a deep oppression weighing on her shoulders. 'So where were we?' she sighed.

Francesco crossed one leg over another and gazed back at her. 'Kate, just what objection do you have to Dominic meeting his grandfather?'

Kate retook her seat. Where should she start? But when she ran it through her head, she realised that most of it was hearsay rather than concrete evidence. How could she explain to Francesco that for seven years, she'd feared the moment when Nico's father learned of Dominic's existence? That she feared he would try to take her son away from her and she'd be left with nothing apart from her memories. It sounded ridiculous. Even she could recognise that.

'I don't want him to,' she said, and knew she sounded like a spoiled child.

'Dominic is a Mazzoni, Kate, whether you like it or not. You can't deny the heritage of the child you conceived. Everything that should have been Nico's will one day be Dominic's.'

Kate ran a finger over the piping at the edge of the chaise longue. She knew that she was losing this argument, yet every instinct screamed at her to keep Dominic and Cesare apart. 'I don't want him to go to Rome,' she said quietly.

'You heard her,' Elizabeth broke in. 'Leave it, Francesco.'

'Oh, for goodness sake!' Francesco rose abruptly to his feet, and Kate caught her breath, wondering what he was going to do. 'Just what do you think I'm suggesting?' He glared at both women. 'Let me make myself clear. A visit. One week. Maybe two. During the child's summer holidays. To meet his grandfather. Please tell me, for it escapes me, what is the harm in that?'

Kate couldn't put it into words. She had a gut instinct. That was all. And until now, she'd never questioned it. She'd held it inside from the night Nico had died, nurtured it, and hadn't even discussed it with her parents. So was she right? She'd never had cause to question it before.

And Francesco sounded so reasonable that her fears appeared ridiculous when put into words. She wavered. Francesco must have sensed her weakness, for it was then that he played his trump card.

'I'd have thought you'd have wanted to visit Rome, Kate.'

'Really?'

Francesco nodded. 'That is where Nico is buried. In the grounds of the Villa Mazzoni.'

'You beast!' she said.

9

Francesco Mazzoni had won. As Kate had always known he would, though she hadn't made it easy for him. Her fears, which she'd nurtured in private for seven years, seemed ludicrous when faced with this man and his cool logical reasoning.

He was also extremely persistent and, like any good salesman, would have continued for as long as it took to clinch the deal. She wondered afterwards if he'd simply worn her down for, instead of feeling defeated, she only felt relief that she was finally going home.

Elizabeth hugged them both as they left. 'Promise me one thing, Francesco.' She grasped him earnestly by the arms. 'You will act as Kate and Dominic's protector during their visit.'

'Protector?' Francesco looked incredulous. 'I will be taking them to our family home, Mama. Not into a war zone.'

Elizabeth retained her grip on her son. 'Nevertheless. Humour me, Francesco.'

'All right. Yes, I promise, Mama. Whatever.' He kissed her on both cheeks and looked grim as he entered the car. Kate waved to Rose, who was watching from an upstairs window, and took her seat beside him.

As soon as the car began its slow progress along the drive, Francesco turned to her. 'It is a long journey home.'

Kate checked her watch and grimaced. Dominic would be fast asleep by the time they got there.

He continued, 'Far too long for you to cover your ears and not hear what I wish to say.'

Kate pulled a face. 'Go on then. If you must.'

'All my life, whatever decisions I have made, whatever action I have taken, I have been able to live with my conscience.'

Kate looked at him. If this was his

idea of an apology, then she definitely would punch him.

'Apart from once, Kate. Once, I acted so extremely and so out of character that my conscience will never forget nor forgive my actions.'

'Oh yeah, as soon as I saw you again I could tell how cut up about it you've been all these years.'

Francesco bowed his head. 'Because I didn't know who you were?'

'Doesn't sort of fit with this person wracked by agonies of conscience, wouldn't you agree?'

'Kate, I wouldn't have recognised you the day afterwards.'

'Gee thanks.'

'I wouldn't have recognised anyone from that night, parts of which are still a horrendous blank. I'd just learned that I'd lost my younger brother and you, unfortunately, took the brunt of all the anger, guilt and grief that I felt. I am deeply ashamed of myself, but I will make it up to you somehow.'

Kate studied him. His voice sounded

sincere, his look genuine, but his speech sounded just a little too rehearsed. That was it, it was the salesman coming to the fore again, probably to allay any remaining fears she might have about a visit to meet Cesare.

'You'll make it up to me?' she murmured. 'Just like you scoured Sussex for me after Nico's death?'

'Francesco looked surprised. 'Who told you that?'

'Your mother. Don't worry, Francesco. I didn't laugh.'

'It was the truth.'

'So why didn't you find me?'

'I came to the conclusion eventually that you didn't want to be found. I spoke to your neighbours, to the police — I even put advertisements in the local newspapers. All I knew was your first name . . . Caterina. Everything I tried drew a blank'.

Kate considered. She had no evidence that he wasn't telling the truth. After that night, all she'd wanted was to get away from the cottage they'd rented that summer. She'd caught the first bus to London, gone to ground in her parents' home and licked her wounds there for a long time.

She propped her elbow on the window ledge and stared at the passing scenery, thinking about what he'd told her. So what was she supposed to say now . . . ? 'It's OK, Francesco, I accept your apology and I forgive you?' Well, no. Maybe a better person than her could say it and mean it, but she couldn't. He'd hurt her too much, and she still didn't trust him.

To his credit, he didn't force the issue. He'd said his bit and seemed content to leave it at that for the present. Or maybe it was that, apology over, his mind had wandered to other matters.

That seemed to be the case when she spoke some time later and he visibly started. 'You mean to tell me that your bad temper has never made you do anything else you've regretted?' she wanted to know.

'I do not have a bad temper,' he enunciated carefully.

Kate gave a snort. 'Oh no, you can't get away with that one. It's me you're talking to, Francesco, remember?'

'I do, and I have apologised. It was an aberration.'

'And what about that poor guy who you were shouting at when I came for my interview? Was that an aberration as well?'

'No that was embezzlement,' he answered coldly. 'I suspected the 'poor guy' the instant I inspected my mother's books, but it took until three o'clock on the morning of your interview before I could prove it. The man was obviously skilled in such matters, so what was I supposed to do? Congratulate him on his talent?'

'OK.' Kate accepted that she couldn't win them all. 'What about those women at the hotel?'

He looked blank for a few moments, then, 'They would try the patience of a saint.'

'And you're no saint, right?'

He gave a long slow smile. 'No, *cara*, I certainly am not.'

'Don't call me that,' she snapped, disturbed by the way the silkiness of his tone reverberated deep within her. Never, ever, would she be *his* darling!

His jaw tightened. 'You would prefer it if I reverted to Miss Thompson?'

'I don't give a monkey's. Just don't call me that.'

He flicked his fingers in a gesture of exasperation. 'So what is the verdict, Kate? Do you accept that I am not generally bad-tempered?'

'The jury's still out. I'll let you know.' She foraged in her bag for her Walkman, and watched his eyebrows rise in surprise as she selected a cassette and switched the machine on. She'd never have dreamed of being so rude with anyone else but, as Rhett Butler once said, frankly she didn't give a damn. He'd got what he wanted — the kudos of being able to present Dominic to his father. She wasn't going to flatter his ego by telling him he was Mr Wonderful. The rock music blasted her brain, and she closed her eyes allowing everything to fade but the beat.

She was mellowing with Dire Straits when he laid a hand on her arm. She took off her earphones. 'We need to talk,' he said, handing her a cheque.

She presumed it was her wages, and wondered why he looked uncomfortable about it. Then she saw the amount scrawled on the cheque. 'What's this?' she demanded.

He didn't meet her gaze. 'It is nothing. You will need money for your visit. New outfits for you and Dominic. There will be other expenses . . . '

Methodically, Kate folded the cheque and handed it back. 'This 'nothing' as you call it, Francesco, happens to be more than I earned last year. You make a great salesman, but you'd be rubbish as a diplomat.'

Francesco stared at the cheque, seeming not to know what to do with it.

'I intended no insult, Kate,' he said quietly.

She shrugged. 'None taken.'

He tried again. 'Then please take it.'

'No. I'll take the money for this job.' She checked her watch. 'Plus overtime, but that's it.'

He sighed. 'Do you hate me so much?'

She evaded the question. 'I prefer to pay my own way. Always have.'

He thought for a moment. 'And with Nico?'

She glared at him, and he raised his hands in defence. 'That was not a trick question, Kate. I'm interested, that's all. Tell me to mind my own business, if you like.'

'With Nico, it was different . . . '

He waited for her to continue.

'He took my money, I took his. It's called sharing. It's called love.'

'I think I understand.' Francesco flashed her a perfect smile. 'So you didn't mind that you would be

159

marrying a rich man?'

Kate laughed. Put that way, the question sounded ridiculous. 'I didn't really think about it. I was eighteen when I met Nico, and I fell head over heels in love. There wasn't much time for thinking.' She smiled as she recalled what they spent most of their time doing when she wasn't working.

To her surprise, Francesco lifted her hand and touched it to his lips. 'My brother was a fortunate man. Once more, I can only offer my apology.'

She stared at him in shock as an electric current surged up her arm. 'We were both fortunate,' she said and pulled away, wondering if he was at all aware of the havoc he'd caused by his simple touch.

He smiled. 'I have a favour to ask. I would like to meet Dominic before our visit to Rome.'

Right. So now she knew the reason for his gallantry — to butter her up ready for his next question. 'Fine. Bring his Aunt Ethel, Uncle Fred, Aunt

Maisie and Auntie Flo. We'll all have a party.'

It took a while before Francesco answered. 'It would be sensible, don't you think, if I am to accompany the boy to Rome, that I should meet him beforehand?'

'Oh yes, we'd better do the sensible thing.' Were they talking about a person now or a business transaction?

He raised his palms in defeat. 'I don't understand, Kate. May I or may I not meet Dominic?'

'Yes.' He was right. It did make sense.

He waited.

'Tuesday. We'll pick him up from school at half past three and take him to the park.'

'Tuesday,' he murmured, and flipped open a personal organiser. She saw from the frown that creased his brow that the time must clash with something, and she wondered if he would try to re-negotiate. She didn't care what day he saw Dominic, but she wasn't

161

going to offer. She watched with interest as the dilemma flickered across his features. He snapped the organiser closed. 'Tuesday.' He smiled. 'I shall look forward to it.'

She smiled back, in congratulation that his nephew meant more to him than a business meeting.

It was a start.

10

At half past three the following Tuesday, she and Francesco stood with the other mothers outside Dominic's school. Even though she'd insisted that Derek should park the Bentley in the next street, Francesco still caused a sensation among them. Dressed in a dark business suit, he'd obviously rushed straight from work, but even dressed in T-shirt and shorts or jogging trousers like the few other men there, she suspected that he'd still cause a minor spectacle. There was just something about the man. He attracted women to him like wasps to a can of Coke. Mothers who'd never given her the time of day before, clearly felt compelled to ask how Dominic was getting on with his new teacher and whether he was looking forward to the summer holidays.

Kate answered them politely, but she might have been answering them in Serbo-Croat for all the notice they took. Their attention was rooted firmly on Francesco and, for once, the man was all smiles and charm, chatting amiably on everything from the weather to Wimbledon.

As the first children launched themselves through the school gates, he turned to her. 'Will we walk to the park from here?'

'If you want to see a six year-old boy cry,' she said, then grinned at the look of astonishment on his face. 'Having a ride in your car has been the sole topic of Dominic's conversation for the past three days.'

'Ah.' She saw the answering smile fade from his eyes to be replaced by a look of shock. When she followed the direction of his gaze, she saw Dominic, head down, running for all his worth towards the school gates in an attempt to beat his friend, Ravi, through them.

'Same every afternoon,' she said,

before realising that she was talking to Francesco's back.

'I'll meet you at the car,' he said, walking stiffly away.

Kate was still staring after him when Dominic cannoned into her. What on earth was so urgent? Some phone call which he'd forgotten to make?

She turned to Dominic and gave him a hug. 'Where's your lunch box?' she asked, and they had to return to the classroom to retrieve it.

As they rounded the corner of the next street, Kate half-expected to see the Bentley gone, and Francesco with it. Her first thought was how to explain the disappointment to Dominic, but close behind came the conviction that if he could let his nephew down like this, then she could quite as easily renege on her promise to take Dominic to Rome.

But standing by the Bentley, with the sunlight gleaming off its paintwork, was Francesco. He'd removed his suit jacket and was in the process of rolling up his shirt sleeves when he spotted them.

Immediately he started towards them, incongruous with one sleeve buttoned and one rolled up.

'Hello, Dominic.' He crouched down and smiled at his nephew, who looked past him towards the Bentley.

'What kind of engine has it got? Mummy didn't know,' he said.

Francesco was about to answer when Kate grabbed Dominic's arm. 'Hello, Uncle Francesco. It's nice to meet you,' she prompted. She had cause to be rude to the man but her son, as yet, did not.

Dominic did as he was bid then immediately repeated his first question. It was answered with a smile and followed by as much information as even Dominic could want. If Francesco was ever made bankrupt, he could always find another job as a mechanic. Derek, too, was all smiles. He lifted Dominic into the front seat and allowed him to grind gears and flick switches to his heart's content.

'So what was so urgent?' she asked.

The horn blasted out part of her question and she signalled Dominic not to do it again.

'I beg your pardon?' Francesco looked at a loss.

'Why did you have to rush back here? Important phone call, was it?'

Disbelief flooded his features. 'You are joking, I hope?'

She didn't answer.

He shook his head in exasperation. 'What is your English expression — 'Big boys don't cry'?' He paused. 'I left because I didn't want to embarrass you in front of your friends by betraying my emotion.'

'I see.' She looked away from the penetrating dark gaze. Once again, he'd succeeded in wrong-footing her, and she had no means of knowing whether or not he was telling the truth. He looked perfectly in control of his emotions at the moment.

They drove to the park, Dominic wide-eyed and alert, every fibre of his being soaking in the experience.

She smiled indulgently, even though Francesco was now relaying statistics about every car he had ever driven. Lord, she hoped he wouldn't keep this up all the way to Rome, and she made a mental note to remember to take her Walkman.

'Shall we continue a little longer?' Francesco enquired as the park came into sight. Dominic turned an earnest face to her, and she smiled her assent.

'What kind of car does Mummy have?' she heard Francesco ask, and she grinned. How was her son ever going to bear the shame of having a mother who couldn't drive?

'Mummy doesn't have a car,' he answered plaintively. 'I don't know why.'

Kate saw the questions formulating in Francesco's mind. Was it that she couldn't drive? Was it money? Was it an environmental issue? She watched him with interest, wondering which one he'd choose.

He wrinkled up his nose. 'London

isn't the nicest place to drive,' he replied, probably congratulating himself on steering out of a minefield.

But he didn't know Dominic. In a heartbeat, the question, 'Why?' shot back at him. She saw him hesitate. Now he had to give her son a satisfactory answer without, at the same time, rubbishing his birthplace. Kate settled back. This was a lot more fun than car specifications.

Finally, they halted outside the park. 'There you go.' Kate handed Francesco a bag of crusts.

He stared at them blankly.

'Packed lunch. Keep you going till dinner-time,' she continued, but couldn't contain her giggles in the face of such utter astonishment. 'Oh for goodness sake, Francesco, don't tell me you've never fed ducks before!'

'Ah.' His eyes twinkled with amusement, then with a more profound emotion as a small hand slipped into his and began tugging him towards the pond.

'There's a really naughty duck, Uncle Francesco. You mustn't throw any bread to him because he eats everybody else's.'

'A bit like your Uncle Francesco,' murmured Kate, watching them head off without a backwards glance. She'd given birth to Dominic, would have laid down her life for him, then along comes Francesco and within less than an hour, he was her son's number one person.

Immediately, Kate told herself not to be such a cow. She ought to be thanking God that Dominic was happy with Francesco. In fact, she must make sure that she never allowed her own feelings about the man to prejudice that relationship in any way.

'Race you to the pond!' she shouted, running after them.

★ ★ ★

A fortnight later, Kate was seated next to Dominic on their flight to Rome. It was the first time he had flown and he was bouncing with excitement. Clutched in his hand was a miniature green Bentley. Francesco had discovered that they'd been unable to buy an exact replica of his car, so he'd had one especially made and presented Dominic with it at Heathrow Airport.

'You are not fond of flying?' From across the aisle, he reached over and touched her arm lightly.

'Not very,' she lied. Her stomach was churning and she felt sick, but it had nothing to do with flight nerves. She dreaded this visit, and no matter how ultra-nice Francesco was being, she wouldn't be happy until they were on the plane home.

'Hold on to my hand, if you like,' he offered, but she shook her head. Her stomach had a tendency to react strangely whenever he inadvertently brushed against her. In its present volatile state, she didn't fancy its chances.

As the plane began its descent into

Fiumicino airport, the flight attendant brought around sweets. Dominic was about to make a grab for them, but Kate waved her away. She caught the glance that Francesco gave her and sighed; it was people's normal reaction.

'I've brought my own.' She fished them out of her bag and popped one into Dominic's mouth. 'He gets hyperactive with certain colours — tartrazine and sunset yellow are the worst.'

'And these substances will be contained in the sweets the flight attendant offered?'

Kate shrugged. 'I couldn't tell you for certain without reading the packet, but I'm not taking any chances.'

Francesco looked unconvinced. 'Nico was also very active as a child.'

Kate gave a start as Dominic crashed his car against the window, and she raised a finger of warning. 'I'll send it to the garage if it doesn't behave.'

Dominic grinned back, and waggled his finger at the Bentley. 'Bad car,' he said.

Kate turned back to Francesco. 'There's active and there's hyperactive. Believe me, once you've witnessed it you'll know the difference.'

He thought for a moment. 'It must be quite a problem for you.'

Kate shook her head. Apart from this, her son was a perfectly normal, perfectly healthy boy. Grateful for this, the problem seemed minuscule. 'I have to be careful, that's all. You wouldn't believe the colourings that some manufacturers put into their food. My speciality is coal-tar dyes, but I must know them all by now. If they ever have a game show called 'Name That Sweet', I'd win a fortune!'

Francesco laughed. He looked over at Dominic, caught his eye and winked. 'I'll make sure that all the staff at the villa are aware,' he said.

It had been hot when they'd left London, but the temperature outside the terminal building made Kate gasp. Dominic had worn himself out with excitement and was now dragging on her arm. 'Not much longer,' she soothed.

'Would you like to ride on my shoulders while we walk to the car?' Francesco turned to them.

'I'm a bit heavy,' she said.

'Mummy!' Dominic squealed with laughter. The mental picture conjured up by her remark had obviously hit the spot.

Francesco lifted her son high into the air and perched him on his wide shoulders. She marvelled as Dominic transformed instantly from limp rag to human dynamo, beating a tattoo on Francesco's chest with his heels and crowing with glee. God, that must hurt. She winced as his trainers slammed backwards and forwards into Francesco's breastbone, but his uncle seemed to be enjoying the experience and showed no sign of discomfort.

He'll be bruised tonight, she thought, then wished she hadn't as her mind displayed, for her edification, the muscular torso of the man, complete with tiny dark marks on his smooth chest.

She'd managed to chase the picture away when they both turned to check that she was following, and her heart contracted. Lord, how similar they looked! Not just the eyes, but also certain gestures that she was beginning to notice. She wondered, not for the first time, if any of her genes had made it into Dominic's physiology. For there could be no doubt whatsoever that Mazzoni blood flowed strongly through the veins of both individuals before her.

They appeared to be heading for a large white car. Kate studied it, trying to recognise its make. Nope, she didn't have a clue. She'd look at the back, where such things were normally written, before she got in so that she didn't appear totally ignorant.

But as the driver smiled at her while opening the passenger door, Kate completely forgot her intention. Oh bliss! The big white car might not have a name, but it had amazing air conditioning. Walking to it, she'd felt like an ice cream melting in the sun.

Kate heard Francesco censure the driver for parking in the wrong place, but there was little conviction in his voice, and he entered the car smiling broadly. 'Isn't this the most wonderful climate?' He gestured at the golden orb above him.

Kate glanced up, then shielded her eyes from the glare. 'Wonderful if you happen to be a solar panel.'

'You don't like the sun?'

'It would be more true to say that it doesn't like me.'

He looked at her carefully. 'I hope you've brought sunscreen,' he said and the corner of his mouth twitched.

'Oh yes.' She knew from his amusement that the tip of her nose must already be a delectable shade of strawberry pink. 'I start off on factor 306, and by the end of the week I should have worked down to factor 303.'

'And Dominic?'

Kate put her arms around her son and hugged him to her as the car moved away. She hoped that the movement would lull him into having a nap. He'd hardly slept last night for excitement. 'Dominic?' she repeated. 'I'll slap a bit of cream on him when I can catch him, make sure he's wearing a hat when it's particularly hot and, in a couple of days, he'll be as brown as you.'

He smiled, then gazed speculatively at the milky whiteness of her arms. 'In time, you would turn a wonderful golden colour, like a lightly-toasted almond.'

'Almond?' Kate snorted. 'Nope. Think Brighton rock, Francesco. White with pink stripes, where I've missed with the cream.'

Instead of laughing, as she'd intended him to, the corners of his lips curved sexily. 'I adore rock,' he murmured.

Only then did it occur to her that candy rock with its connotations of mouths and sweet stickiness was altogether the wrong analogy. 'Or think deck chairs with their pink-and-white stripes,' she attempted.

His dark eyes glowed like embers. 'I much prefer rock,' he said silkily, assuring her that he knew exactly what track her mind had taken and he was right there beside her.

Kate felt the betrayal of her body, and was glad that Dominic was lying against her and hiding the evidence of the hardening peaks of her breasts. God, this man was dangerous! It had been a mistake to believe she was immune. Then she realised that he was playing with her, and her immunity was restored. Deprived of his usual female company for a week, he was amusing himself by practising on her.

Kate felt Dominic grow heavy and she settled him more comfortably on her lap, stroking his hair until he finally gave in and fell asleep. His face relaxed into a picture of angelic innocence that only young children can create, and which she never tired of watching. It would disappear soon enough as he grew, never to be recaptured.

She looked up to find Francesco gazing at them. 'Isn't he gorgeous?' She smiled.

'Absolutely.' He continued staring at them. 'Mother and child,' he murmured. 'I wish at this moment that I had my mother's talent.'

After a steep climb, the car slowed before a pair of immense iron gates, which slowly swung open to allow them entry. The gatekeeper waved to them as they passed through, and she stared back at him. 'Don't say we're here already?' she demanded.

'Why not?'

'Because I wouldn't have let him go to sleep if I'd known,' she said, making an effort to soften her tone. Francesco wasn't to know that twenty minutes wasn't enough to refresh Dominic, but was quite enough to make him ratty when he was woken.

'You wish him to have longer?'

'It would have been better.'

He considered. 'Perhaps you would like to stay with him in the car for a while longer?'

'I could give it a try,' she said, but knew that there was little hope of Dominic remaining asleep. In this she was proved right. As soon as the car stopped, Dominic's head shot up, but thankfully with the other she was proved wrong and he appeared as bright as if he'd slept for hours.

'Is this where grandpapa lives?' he asked, scrambling to his feet and trying to clamber over her to look out of the window.

'Indeed it is.' Francesco smiled at him.

Indeed it was. Since her anxiety on the plane, she'd managed to blot it out, but the solid presence of the Villa Mazzoni before them made that impossible. She looked up at the ochre-and-russet fortress and her stomach tied in knots. She wanted to run away. If she'd been able to drive, she'd have bundled

Dominic back into the car and made her escape. She was terrified, and she started to talk about anything and everything.

'Did I ever tell you how difficult it was to get Dominic to sleep when he was a baby?' she said, focusing on Francesco's rather startled expression rather than the main entrance to the villa that he was leading her to.

'I've heard some people saying that they would take their baby for a drive in the car to get them to sleep, my friend used to walk hers in the park for hours, but I used to put a load of washing in the machine and put Dominic on top of it.' She giggled. 'On top of the machine, of course, not on top of the washing.' She could hear the hysterical rise in her voice, but was unable to control it. She was dimly aware of people smiling at her and cooing at Dominic as they passed, but was unable to respond.

'Sometimes that machine was on three times a night; I must have had the cleanest clothes in Hounslow,' she

181

continued doggedly. 'It had a vicious spin cycle, but Dominic always slept through it. Probably dreaming he was in Formula One.'

'Kate.' They stopped before an intricately-carved wooden door. 'Kate,' he repeated, forcing her to look up at him. 'It's going to be all right. I promise.' He laid both hands on her shoulders and squeezed gently. She wondered why his hands were shaking, then realised it was her own trembling that was causing it.

'Do you want to leave this meeting until later?'

She stepped away from him and took a deep breath. 'No, let's get it over with.'

11

Was this the man of whom she'd been so afraid?

His penetrating gaze met hers as she walked into the room and she realised that yes . . . the eyes were the same, and she would have known him to be a Mazzoni. But what about the rest? Where was his sons' aristocratic bearing, their grace, or their presence? It was a shock to realise that all such attributes had been inherited from their mother.

She wanted to laugh. Not at him, but at herself. She couldn't be afraid of this short hunched man; he resembled nothing more than a hungry old crow. Perhaps her lips did twitch as the thought flitted through her mind, because his stare became even more malevolent. Oh yes, if looks could kill, they'd be ringing for an ambulance right now.

Beside her, Francesco was making introductions. He could have saved his breath. They both knew who the other was, and Cesare wasn't taking the slightest notice of his son. That was strange. All the other Italians she knew would have been hanging on each other's necks and doing the kissing thing by now.

Kate felt a pull on her arm. Dominic was starting to fidget and had his eye on an overfed Persian cat lying on the back of an armchair. She tightened her grip on his hand — the cat didn't seem too pleased to see them either as its tail swished back and forth in warning.

'And this is Dominic.' Dominic heard his name and pulled free. She'd coached him what to say to his grandfather, and he was keen to say his party piece.

She watched with pride as he strode confidently towards the old man. Lord, where had that arrogant swagger come from? Then she watched with interest for Cesare's reaction.

It was some time coming. At first Cesare just stared at him, his expression unreadable. Dominic, who'd been told that his grandfather would probably try to hug him, shake his hand or say something first, grew impatient. His head swivelled back to her, his expression clearly asking — have I got the right man?

Kate nodded and gestured to her son just to get on with it. Dominic turned back to the old man and stuck out his hand. When Cesare failed to respond, Dominic grabbed his hand and shook it up and down. '*Buongiorno, Nona, come sta?*' he said, and turned back to her with a look of delight that he'd remembered what to say.

His grandson's greeting seemed to jolt Cesare from his inertia. The hard coarsened features crumbled and, with a cry that invoked most of the known saints, the old man dropped to his knees. Like a Venus fly trap, Cesare's arms shot out and ensnared Dominic, who let out a squeal before he realised that this was all part of what he'd been told might happen.

Kate's heart softened as she saw the tears in the old man's eyes. He couldn't be that bad if he was able to show emotion like this. Maybe he had reason to hate her. Hadn't she kept a living memory of his son away from him all these years? Maybe she should apologise? She bit her lip. Maybe she should wait and see how the week turned out.

Dominic started to struggle. He'd been extremely good and had lasted much longer than she expected. When Cesare let him go, she held out her hand and crouched down. 'Clever boy! You remembered it all,' she praised.

Dominic wrinkled his nose. 'He smells funny.'

'Shh!' According to Francesco, his father spoke little English. She hoped this was the case.

Francesco laid a hand on her shoulder and with the other one, ruffled Dominic's hair. 'I'll show you to your rooms.' He smiled.

'One moment, Francesco.' Cesare's voice boomed out with authority. There was no trace of moisture in his eyes as he walked over to her. 'I want to have a closer look at the woman responsible for Nico's death.'

Kate's heart started to thud. 'Why should you think that, Signor Mazzoni?'

'Why?' She and Cesare were about the same size and, as he spoke, a tiny globule of spit landed on her cheek. She shuddered and wiped it away. 'Why?' he repeated. 'If it wasn't for you, Nico would have been at home, safe in Italy.'

'It was an accident, Papa.' Francesco's voice and expression were grave as he put his arm around his father's shoulders and pulled him away from her. 'This is no way to speak to a guest in our home. Please apologise to Kate.'

'Apologise? I'll go to my grave before I'll apologise! Nico would have been alive today if that whore hadn't lain on her back every night and kept him away from me.'

Kate's mouth dropped open and she was too shocked to respond. Francesco remonstrated with his father to little effect. Seven years of hate were stored in the old man. The sewer gates were now open and it all spewed out.

It was Dominic clinging to her legs that spurred her into action. It was something he hadn't done since his first day at school and it was something she hadn't expected to see again. 'It's OK,' she soothed, as he lifted his frightened face up towards her. She scooped him into her arms and walked out of the room, leaving the two men battling with one another.

She headed for the first room where she could hear the sound of voices, and swept the door open. 'Please direct us to our room,' she commanded one of the startled maids, who promptly obeyed.

And now what? Kate set Dominic on his feet and gazed around. It was a beautiful room, looking out over a cobbled courtyard and fountain. Idyllic in any other circumstances.

'I like my other grandpa best,' Dominic informed her and, even though she'd promised herself faithfully that she wouldn't try to influence him, Kate dropped a kiss on his head and agreed with him.

'Why was he shouting?'

Because he's a stupid old man. Incredibly stupid, frightening a six-year-old like that. She noticed that Dominic still hadn't moved from her side. Normally he'd be investigating everything, while she'd be following to make sure that he couldn't harm himself.

She knelt down, but kept her thoughts to herself. 'He was upset about something. It wasn't you.' She gave Dominic a bright smile. 'He thought you were great. He wouldn't have given you such a big cuddle if he hadn't.'

Dominic thought for a moment. 'Was

he upset with Uncle Francesco?'

Kate nodded. 'Yes, but Uncle Francesco will be OK.' She stood up. 'Right, let's go and see if this is your room through here.' She pushed open a door. 'Oh yes, brilliant.' Beside a bed covered in a racing car duvet was a cupboard bursting with new toys and games. That should keep Dominic occupied for as long as it took.

'They're for you to play with,' she encouraged, and had to smile at the look of puzzlement on his face. Nobody told me it was Christmas, it seemed to say. She did a quick check of the window. Nope, he couldn't open that, and no balcony to throw himself off, and she headed for the door. 'I'm just in the next room,' she said, but there was no reply. Dominic was busy opening boxes.

She'd just picked up the phone when there was a knock at the door. Hell! She'd expected Francesco to be much longer.

But it wasn't Francesco. It was a

maid. She looked about thirteen. 'I've come to unpack.' She picked up a case and started to open it.

'No thanks.' Kate laid her hand over the girl's to stop her. There wasn't any point unpacking when they were leaving on the next plane.

The girl stared at her, undecided.

'I like to do it myself,' said Kate, and steered her out of the door before she could protest.

She returned to the phone, trailed her finger down the telephone directory and dialled the number. The woman on the other end was extremely helpful, patiently waiting while Kate jotted down times and prices. 'Yes, I'd like to book that one.' Kate dug out her credit card. Pity she hadn't had the foresight to ask Francesco for their return tickets. They'd be travelling to Heathrow in considerably less style than they'd left.

'4060 . . . ' Kate confirmed the numbers on her card, then waited for the transaction to complete. Poor card. It had been through more machines in the last week than it had been in its lifetime.

And for what? Kate glared at the cases that were stuffed with the new clothes she'd bought for her and Dominic so that they wouldn't look too out of place in Nico's house. By next summer, Dominic would have out-grown them, and when was she going to need all those posh frocks?

Kate rapped her credit card up and down on the desk. She shouldn't have been so vain. She should have stuck to her first intention and travelled here only with what they had already. It wouldn't have made one iota of difference to the reception she'd received from Cesare Mazzoni.

And what about this added expense? Despairingly, Kate stared at the figure she'd jotted down. When they got back, she'd have to sign up with some more agencies and take anything they offered.

'Come on.' Kate shifted the phone to her other ear. Had the woman gone on her coffee break and forgotten about her? Seconds later, the piped music ceased and a female voice crackled down the line.

'There must be some mistake,' she said when the woman told her that her credit card had been refused. 'No, I haven't any other means of payment.' She bit her lip. 'Do you think you could check again?' she asked, but the woman had already gone.

At first, paranoia suggested that Cesare had been at work, tampering with her finances, then her gaze took in the cases in the corner of the room. With an almighty kick, she sent one of them hurtling into the centre. It was their fault, or at least the clothes in them. If they hadn't asked to be bought, she wouldn't have reached her credit limit.

But there was nobody to blame but herself. She sank on to the floor and rested her head on her case.

So what was she to do? She gnawed at her prize fingernail. Someone like her didn't deserve to display such perfection. There, it was off, and she stared at its jagged edge with dismay.

Where was she to get some money? Apart from pinching one of the Old Masters from the walls and trying to fence it in Rome, there didn't seem to be too many options.

Her parents? Kate propped her elbows on her knees and rested her head in her hands. Yes, they'd bail her out in a heartbeat. But the results of her dad's last check-up had been worrying, and the doctors were having difficulty controlling his blood pressure. 'Try to avoid stress of any sort, Mr Thompson,' they'd told him. He'd been so pleased for her 'going off on this lovely little holiday'. What was he going to think if she rang him up the same day wanting a ticket home?

Her friends? She'd always believed herself fortunate in having plenty of those, but how many could she ask for that amount of money? She did a quick survey and shook her head. Forget it.

There was a knock at the door, and

Kate sighed as she got up to answer it. Francesco walked in, and she saw that whatever had passed between the two men since her absence had left its mark. He looked like a man deprived of sleep for two days. Good. She'd always believed in sharing. If she was suffering, then he could have some too.

'How can I apologise, Kate?' he began.

'You open your mouth and say sorry,' she snapped.

'I'm sorry.' His dark eyes begged forgiveness. 'I promise you that it won't happen again.'

'Promise?' Her voice screeched out, and she consciously lowered it. 'I seem to recall you promising that everything was going to be hunky dory with your dad not so long ago. I'm sorry, Francesco, but I'm up to here with your promises!'

Two streaks of red flashed across his cheekbones. 'Perhaps if I tried to explain . . . '

Hearing the sound of voices,

Dominic came out of his room. He grabbed her hand, wanting to show her something he'd made. She turned back to Francesco as he pulled her away. 'Forget it, I'm not interested.'

'Is there anything I can do?' he enquired when Dominic was once again settled.

It was worth a try.

'A couple of weeks ago, you offered me some money. I was a bit hasty refusing it. Can I change my mind?'

He raised his eyebrows, and a second later he was staring at her cases with pursed lips. 'May I ask the reason for your sudden change of heart?' he stalled. Anybody who ever thought this man was stupid was in for a nasty surprise.

'You're looking at them.' She gave an airy wave at her cases. 'I went a bit mad in Oxford Street and my bank manager hasn't recovered yet.'

He smiled. 'It would give me the greatest of pleasure to settle your finances, Kate. Give me the details and

196

I will attend to it during your stay.'

She crossed her arms. There was no point pretending. 'You'd keep me here against my will?'

He raked a hand through his hair and sat down. 'No, Kate, I would not.'

'Fine, then how about handing over our return tickets?'

'At least leave it until tomorrow. You're overwrought. Dominic is exhausted.'

'Don't you dare make me feel guilty about my son! Dominic will be fine — he'll sleep on the plane.'

'I apologise.' Francesco stood up and walked to the window. He rested an arm against it and stared out.

'I want to leave,' she repeated.

He turned and looked at her. For a moment, he looked like Dominic did when she told him that he couldn't have a particular toy until his birthday.

'Can you blame me?'

He shook his head.

'So?'

'So you'd leave without visiting Nico's grave?'

Kate closed her eyes as anger imploded in her brain. She waited until it stopped before opening them again.

'Nothing is too low for you to use, is it? All you care about is getting your own way.'

He shook his head. 'You're wrong, Kate. I'm beginning to care very much about you and Dominic.'

And if she believed that, she was an even greater fool than he thought she was.

But she did want to visit Nico.

Dominic burst through the door. 'Toilet!' he demanded, with such urgency that Kate sprung to her feet and ushered him immediately into the ensuite bathroom. He emerged a few minutes later with a big grin on his face and headed back to his room. She caught up with him, turned him round and marched him back to the bathroom.

'Wash your hands,' she said, and

198

supervised the procedure before letting him go.

Francesco looked puzzled. 'How did you know he hadn't?' he asked.

Kate shrugged. 'I just did.' If he had remembered, he'd be waggling his hands in the air and announcing the fact.

'I haven't offered you any refreshment.'

'No, you haven't. Terrible host.' He could take that as a joke or as a criticism. She didn't care which.

'Coffee?' He remained impassive.

She nodded. 'And a bottle of gin.' If she was going grave visiting, she'd need something to fortify her.

He hesitated.

'Coffee will do. And fresh orange juice diluted with water for Dominic, please.'

He picked up the phone and relayed their order.

'A bit like the drive-through at McDonald's,' she said, but he didn't have a clue what she was talking about.

She knew that his offer of coffee was delaying tactics but she was gasping for a drink. The liquid was hot and strong, without any trace of bitterness. Perfect.

She raised her cup in a toast to Francesco. 'Best thing about your house so far,' she told him.

He smiled. It was becoming a lot more difficult to provoke him. 'Will you stay?' he asked.

'No.'

'If you don't accept my promises any longer, then accept my father's. Believe me, he does not offer them lightly, and he undertakes to be nothing but civil to you throughout this week. There will be no repeat of his recent performance, I assure you.'

'Oh yeah? And this was when you took your foot off his throat, was it?'

Francesco stared at her for a second, then turned away to mask his laughter.

'Forgive me, Kate, this is a serious matter.' He turned back, his eyes sparkling. 'You continually surprise me. I really don't believe I've ever met anyone quite like you.'

'It's called progress and not repeating your mistakes,' she drawled. 'They chucked away the mould after me.'

'I do admire the way you seek out the humour in any situation.'

'And I admire the way you waste time flattering me, hoping that all the planes will have lifted off before I notice the time.'

He coloured. 'I meant everything that I said.'

She nodded. 'Course you did.'

He stood up. 'Then we should hurry matters along.'

'We should indeed.' She took a last gulp of coffee before rising to her feet.

'And Dominic?' he enquired softly.

Kate pulled a face. She couldn't leave him here by himself, but how was she going to react at Nico's grave? It wasn't fair to upset him again today. And it would if he saw her crying.

'Perhaps it would be better to leave him in the care of one of the nannies,' Francesco suggested.

Kate looked at him.

'One of the garden rooms has been converted into a playroom and I have employed a team of nannies for the week.'

'A team?' she echoed.

'Fully trained,' he assured her. 'I checked their references personally.'

Kate started to laugh. The man was priceless. She wondered what would happen if Dominic expressed a desire to ice skate. Would he flood one of the downstairs rooms and freeze it for him?

'I fail to see what amuses you,' he said stiffly.

'Don't worry about it.' She smiled up at him. 'It's brilliant, Francesco, thanks. We'll leave him there.'

He caught her by the arms and held her gently. 'Will you at least stay until tomorrow?'

Kate's heart thudded. It wasn't fear. She knew that he would let her go immediately if she struggled. 'I can't, Francesco.' Momentarily, she laid her head on his chest, but it felt too nice and she lifted it. 'Your dad might have promised to be civil to me, but I couldn't with him. I couldn't bear to be in the same room with him again. I'd be done for assault.'

'And if I arranged that you never should? That as far as possible you never had contact with each other?' As he spoke, he rubbed rhythmically up and down her arms. The action was soothing rather than erotic. She felt it lulling her, as she suspected he meant it to, into weak submission.

'I'll think about it.' She pulled away. 'Let's get this over with first. I'm getting really uptight about it.' That had to explain the strange quivering sensation in her stomach.

'Let us go.'

12

Nico's grave was not the huge marble monstrosity that Kate would have expected Cesare to have built for his son, but a simple grass mound on the edge of a hill with a marble cross as a headstone. She hadn't thought to bring flowers, but saw that there was a vase overflowing with lilies under the cross. 'This is lovely.' There was a slight catch to her voice, but she thought she'd be able to keep her emotions under control.

'My father picks fresh flowers and places them there every morning,' Francesco informed her, which was another surprise. She couldn't imagine that hard coarse man doing anything so noble.

'This was Nico's favourite spot as a child. The Circus Maximus used to be held there in ancient times.' Francesco pointed down the hill. 'And Nico used to spend hours up this tree imagining he was taking part in the chariot races.'

Kate laughed. 'Sounds about right.' She looked up at the tree which shaded the grave. Even in the fiercest sun, it would only receive dappled sunlight.

She knelt down by the grave and placed her hand on the warm grass. 'Hello you,' she murmured, forcing herself to imagine Nico as he was, and not how he would be below.

'I've brought you a present,' she whispered, 'but you can't have it until tomorrow.' She paused, taken aback. So she had decided to stay until then? Well, now she knew.

'I like your grass.' She ran her hand over the velvet smooth turf. 'Do you mind if I sit on it?' As there seemed to be no objection, she shuffled over.

'Your present? He's gorgeous, Nico. Best thing we ever did.' She closed her eyes and imagined her lover close but, instead of entwining her in his arms as she was wanted him to, he was nagging at her to give him his present. She opened her eyes and burst out laughing. Francesco, who had been discreetly standing some distance away, moved closer. He probably thought she'd lost it, and was waiting to drag her away.

But it was so funny. And so apt. Nico couldn't wait for anything. If he discovered she'd bought a bottle of wine for the weekend he had to drink it on Tuesday, and when she'd bought him an Easter egg, he'd eaten it the week before.

Kate gazed affectionately at his headstone. This was a first. For the first time ever in their relationship, she had the upper hand. 'And I'll tell you another first,' she spluttered, as the most inappropriate of thoughts struck her. At the time she thought it was hilarious, but afterwards her cheeks burned when she thought what she'd said. 'This is the first time you've ever allowed me on top.'

When she'd recovered from her fit of laughter, she noticed that Francesco had moved away again. 'I've offended your brother,' she told Nico, even though she knew Nico would not have been at all amused by what she'd said. 'You didn't have much of a sense of humour, did you love?' she said, and felt tears prick her eyes. The inscription on the marble blurred as she stared at it. 'In fact, we didn't have much in common at all, did we?' she asked, before the tears flowed.

She cried for a life foreshortened, for a son who would never know his father, and for lost love. Lost forever, because it had never really existed, except in her mind. She would never know about Nico. Perhaps he did love her, as much as he was capable of loving anyone, but with the passage of years she recognised her love for what it was — infatuation. She'd worshipped Nico, but adoration was not a solid foundation for marriage.

Her tears turned to sobs as she tried to come to terms with her new discovery. What had possessed her to hold on so long to the myth that they were a modern day Romeo and Juliet? If he'd lived, they'd have been at each other's throats by now.

Another flood of tears followed.

She supposed that his untimely death had sealed her in a time warp. It had been a way of coping, of dealing with the nightmare she found herself in. 'I'm sorry, Nico.' She touched his headstone lightly as she struggled to her feet. It was an apology that she wouldn't be grieving for him again.

Francesco looked serious as he walked towards her. Was it a trick of the light or were his eyes glistening? 'I am so very sorry, Kate.' To her shock, he enfolded her in his arms. 'I didn't know how much you loved my brother.'

It had been a long time since Kate had been crushed in a man's arms. She felt breathless and started to tremble.

'It's all right,' he reassured, holding her closer until she could hear the rhythmic thud of his heart through the soft cotton of his shirt. This time, she did lay her head on his chest and breathe in the heady perfume of his warm masculine scent. She knew she was there under false pretences, that he would cast her away if he guessed her true feelings, but the shocks of the day had weakened her and she was unable to deny herself this one pleasure.

'All right now?' He extricated himself gently.

No. All she wanted was to snuggle straight back against him. She couldn't believe how bereft she felt. 'I'm fine,' she said.

She noticed the black mascara stains she'd left behind on his shirt. 'Oh God, I must look like a panda!'

Smiling, he brushed gently down her cheek with his knuckles. 'A very lovely panda.' He handed her a handkerchief and waited until she'd wiped the dark smears from her face before they walked back to the house.

Kate wrestled with her conscience. Should she tell Francesco the truth about her discovery? She'd been brought up to tell the truth, the whole truth and nothing but the truth, and it was a creed she generally tried to live by, but what purpose would it serve? She'd feel better if she came clean, but wouldn't it be kinder to Francesco if he retained the illusion that, during his short life, his brother had enjoyed a perfect love?

It probably wasn't the best emotional state to be in when she entered the playroom and found the man she hated encouraging Dominic to stuff himself with sweets. She didn't know how many were in the packet when he'd started, but there were only a few left. Scanning the ingredients, she groaned. Yep, there were E102, E110, and a whole cocktail of others. Dominic would be swinging from the chandeliers tonight.

She turned to Cesare and blazed contempt. 'Were you born without a brain or did you lose it somewhere along the way?' She couldn't believe he'd be so stupid. Or was it that he thought she was lying about his grandson's adverse reaction to colourings and wanted to test for himself? She told him what she thought of that, and watched his face blotch purple with anger. She would have liked to tell him more, but he turned on his heel and walked stiffly out of the room.

Only then did she become aware of Francesco holding her arm and trying to calm her down. 'Come outside,' he said, and led her into the garden.

She leaned against a crumbling brick wall and breathed deeply until the heavy metal beat of her heart decreased to easy listening level. Francesco stuck his hands in his pockets and kicked intermittently at a huge stone urn beside him. 'If you wish to scream at anyone, please scream at me. In private.'

Kate stared at him. She might be slow on the uptake with certain things, but she'd registered the criticism in his tone loud and clear. 'And what was I supposed to do when I saw your dad doing his best to make Dominic ill?

Send him a letter registering my disapproval?' Her voice dripped with sarcasm.

'He was not to blame, Kate. I was.'

And how do you make that out?'

'I did not advise him of Dominic's allergy.'

Kate swore at him.

He waited for a second. 'If you recall, we were discussing other matters.'

Then something struck her. 'But I heard you telling those women before we left.'

He nodded. 'The staff are aware, yes.'

'And they didn't stop him?'

Francesco raised his eyebrows in agreement.

'They're that scared of him?'

Francesco shrugged. 'I cannot explain it, Kate.'

'Oh I think I can.' Third-world dictators probably phoned Cesare Mazzoni for advice.

Francesco straightened up. 'I shall dismiss them all,' he said resignedly.

'No.' She gave a deep sigh. 'They

212

seem to be nice girls. Just make sure that they don't do it again.'

He nodded. 'I shall ensure it.'

When they returned to the playroom, Dominic was playing snakes and ladders with one of the nannies. He hadn't yet seen her and she watched his behaviour closely. Apart from thudding the counter down a little too hard on the board, he seemed OK. Perhaps he was beginning to grow out of this food intolerance. It would be nice.

Suddenly his voice squealed out, 'No! I don't want to go down the snake!' and the board, counters and dice flew into the air. In this mood, if Dominic couldn't win then nobody else was going to.

Kate took a deep breath and let it out slowly. 'Here comes the fun.'

Dominic saw her and raced over. 'Mummy! Mummy! I've played with the truck and I've done you a picture and I spilled all the sand on the floor.' The words came tumbling out, and Kate recognised the familiar spaced-out expression that accompanied them.

'How about a cuddle for Mummy?' She made a grab for him, but he was too quick for her and ran over to one of the girls who was offering him a teddy bear. With a laugh that came straight from Hammer House of Horror, he dropped it on to the floor and set about using it as a football.

'What can I do?' asked Francesco.

'Not a lot.' She followed Dominic's progress with her gaze as she spoke. He soon became bored with his teddy bear football and started bouncing up and down on a mini trampoline in the corner. 'It'll wear off eventually if he doesn't eat any more. The main thing is to stay calm. It does absolutely no good shouting at him.'

'I wouldn't dream of it.'

Kate was sceptical. He might think differently if Dominic started kicking him. She was grateful for the nannies' help. They were showing him different toys and managing to keep him distracted. As soon as she saw him begin to flag, she would grab him, take him away from all stimulation and attempt to calm him down.

'Dominic!' Kate jumped as Francesco's voice thundered around the room. So much for not dreaming of shouting at him. Then she saw Dominic try to bite one of the girls.

'OK, you can go now. Thanks for your help,' she said, and shooed them away. She was on her own.

Not quite. Francesco had picked Dominic up and, despite her son struggling like a wild animal, was holding him and talking to him gently. 'I think we'll go for a walk. I want to show you where your daddy used to play. He used to have a tree house in the orchard.'

Kate caught his arm. 'For God's sake, don't take him into a tree house.'

He winced as Dominic's toe caught him in a sensitive area. 'Trust me, I'm not that stupid.'

She followed, and was taken on a guided tour of the Mazzoni grounds. As they walked Francesco talked, with both actions executed in a slow deliberate fashion. At the beginning, Dominic struggled violently but, as Francesco was much the stronger of the two and held him fast, he gradually became aware of the futility of his actions.

After an hour's tramping in the fading light of the day, Kate saw her son's eyes close. 'He's going to sleep,' she whispered, and Francesco lifted him higher up his chest to make him more comfortable. Dominic clasped his uncle around the neck and his body grew limp.

'Oh thank you,' breathed Kate.

Francesco turned to look at her.

She grinned at him. 'I was giving thanks to the Almighty, but you can have some too.'

He smiled. 'It was the very least I could do.'

'Beyond the call of duty,' she said generously.

'I don't think that I have ever felt so

exhausted.' He gave a rueful grin. 'My back aches, my arms ache, and my body feels as though it's been in a heavyweight boxing competition.'

She giggled. 'Wimp. He's only six.'

He began to laugh, and Dominic stirred. 'No, don't make me laugh.' He patted Dominic on the back until he settled again. 'Will he remain asleep?'

'God, I hope so! He'd normally be going strong until the early hours, but considering the day he's had and the lack of sleep last night, I think he might go through the night.'

'And tomorrow?'

'It depends. Maybe a bit grumpy or a bit clingy.' She shrugged. 'Or he might be fine.'

Francesco gazed at the small figure of his nephew curled on his chest. 'Sleep well, young man,' he whispered, and dropped a kiss on to his cheek.

Kate was startled by his tenderness. Bringing up Dominic on her own had been difficult, but it was no more difficult for her than for thousands of other women in her position. Francesco's gesture, however, had made her realise what she could never give her son — a father's love. There was nothing she could do about that, but it still filled her with an immense sadness. In the gathering darkness, she blinked away the tears.

'Kate? What's wrong?' There was the same softness of tone in his voice as was previously directed towards her son.

Hastily, Kate brushed an arm across her eyes. Did this man miss nothing? 'Oh you know . . . ' She made a vague gesture. 'It's been a long day. I'm shattered.'

'And hungry.' He pushed open a side door of the villa and, to accentuate his point, the wonderful aroma of garlic, herbs, and roasting meat assaulted her nostrils. A woman approaching with a large tureen paused and stared at her blatantly for several seconds before continuing on.

Kate ran a hand through her hair. 'I must look as if Cesare's cat's dragged me round the garden a couple of times.'

He gazed at her speculatively. 'I am certain that you don't.'

Kate smiled. The Italian male might be the most infuriating person on this planet, but they had one redeeming feature. You might know that you looked like a bag lady, but they'd still tell you that you looked lovely.

They reached her room. 'I shall arrange for someone to sit with Dominic so that you can come downstairs. We shall dine together.'

Kate shook her head. 'No, I'd better stay here. Dominic will want me if he wakes up.'

'Then I shall arrange for food to be brought up.' He paused to make sure this was acceptable before adding, 'We shall dine on your balcony.'

The words 'no thanks' sprang to her lips. She was feeling slightly fragile and the last thing she needed was Francesco's supercharged masculine presence, reminding her what she was missing in life.

But the man was being nice. Even now he was lying Dominic gently on the bed and loosening his trainers. He looked up at her. 'Pyjamas?'

Kate shook her head. 'I'm not going to chance messing him about. He can sleep in his clothes tonight. It won't do him any harm.'

Francesco nodded, gently eased the duvet from under Dominic and covered him with it.

Kate was impressed. 'Do you fancy doing some baby-sitting next time you're in London?'

The generous proportions of his mouth widened. 'I would be delighted.'

She'd meant it as a joke, but the thought struck her like a smack on the head that, after witnessing Francesco's behaviour with her son, there was no one she would rather trust with him. Lord, they'd come a long way. If a fortune teller had told her only a month ago that she'd be thinking such things, she'd have demanded her money back!

'I will return in half an hour.' Casting

one last glance at her sleeping son, Francesco hurried to the door.

She stared after him, bemused. Had she actually accepted his dinner invitation? She couldn't remember, so she would give him the benefit of the doubt. Half an hour would give her time to have a quick shower and refresh herself.

It wasn't until she walked over to retrieve clothes from her case that she realised it wasn't there. If she'd been in a hotel she'd have panicked that someone had stolen it, but not here. She knew exactly what had happened. She walked over to the wardrobe, opened the door, and slammed it shut. At what point during that afternoon had Francesco given orders for their cases to be unpacked? Once Dominic had eaten the sweets it was evident that they had to stay, but was it before then? Apart from asking him, there was no way of knowing.

And just when she thought he was being nice.

Nice? Huh! To Francesco, nice was one of the means you used in order to get your own way. She'd do well to remember it.

She was still drying her hair when there was a knock at the door and Francesco appeared with a trolley of food. It was either raining outside or he'd taken the opportunity, like her, of a quick shower. His dark hair was still damp and he smelled enticingly of a mixture of shampoo, shower-gel and after-shave.

She unplugged the hairdryer and fluffed her hands through her hair. It would have to do. As she wrapped the flex around the handle, she caught sight of her reflection in the mirror and immediately behind, she caught sight of Francesco watching her. She'd wondered what his reaction to this royal-blue backless dress would be. It was suitably gratifying. She'd bought it so was determined to wear it. Maybe she could change halfway through the meal into one of the others so she could get the use out of that one as well.

'I compliment you, Kate.' His voice was little more than a purr.

'Oh?' She turned to face him, and he surveyed the front of her dress as blatantly as he'd done the back.

'Most women of my acquaintance would have taken hours and still not succeeded in looking as beautiful as you.'

Kate let out a cackle. She looked good but not that good. Her hair was wondering where the tongs were and she didn't have a scrap of make-up on. But, despite the fact that she'd intended remaining cross with him, his words had lifted her spirits. 'Flattery thy name is Francesco,' she murmured, and pushed past him. 'Let's see what's on your trolley then.'

Sitting high up on the Aventine, one of the original seven hills that Rome was built on, with the lights of the city twinkling below, had to rate as the best place she'd ever eaten. Kate kicked off her sandals, shifted a patio chair closer and rested her feet on it.

'Ever thought of opening a restaurant up here, Francesco?' she murmured. 'You'd make a brilliant waiter.'

Francesco smiled, and bent over to pick up another bottle of wine while she admired his back view.

'You've got . . . ' she began, before stopping herself sharply. That wine was potent. She'd very nearly told Francesco Mazzoni that he had the perfect butt for a waiter! 'Not for me, thanks,' she said, as he made to refill her glass. 'I think I've had plenty.'

He retook his seat and sipped his drink. Francesco, after their meal, looked as sleek and satisfied as a sated pussy cat.

Pussy cat? Kate's mouth curved. Substitute jaguar or cheetah, after a successful kill. She glanced over at him. Shouldn't he be lining her up for the kill by now? But at the moment he was lost in his own thoughts, gazing into the distance.

She'd enjoyed their evening. He'd

told her very little about himself, she realised, but encouraged her to talk about her life and especially about her son. It was a rare indulgence. Conscious that to most people, other people's children were marginally less interesting than holiday videos, Kate had never spoken so much about Dominic.

So there it was. She was wined, dined and flattered to perfection. Wasn't it now time to broach the subject he'd been so assiduously avoiding all evening? She lifted her feet from the chair and scraped it away. It brought Francesco back from whatever planet he was visiting.

'I'm sorry, you were saying . . . ?' He looked startled.

'I was saying . . . ' She hesitated for several moments before making up her mind. 'I was saying that you have a lovely home, Francesco.'

He looked grave. 'Perhaps now I can persuade you to spend longer in it.'

Disappointment surged through her.

It was ridiculous. She'd offered him the perfect opening, so why should she feel so gutted when he'd grabbed it?

He was gazing at her, trying to judge her reaction, but she kept her expression blank when she looked up at him. It was getting easier. There was a lot to be said from learning from the best.

'I've cleared my diary completely for this week,' he continued.

OK, that impressed her. She knew it would take some doing. It would also get right up his nose if all his effort was in vain.

'I want to show Rome to you and Dominic. We will visit wherever you choose.' He looked at her, but again no reaction. 'I want to show you and Dominic where Nico grew up.'

Kate picked up her glass, realised she'd drunk it all and put it down again. A little below the belt, Francesco.

'There will be no repeat of today's performance, and you may supervise personally everything Dominic eats.'

Yep, she certainly would.

'What do you say, Kate?'

She'd say that he could have tried harder. This wasn't quite the hard sell she'd expected. 'I say that I'm tired. I want to go to bed.' She stood up.

He rose to his feet, his expression confused. Was she or was she not going to stay?

Kate stifled a yawn. Her brain was fuddled with alcohol and the need for sleep. She'd give him his answer in the morning. When she knew it herself.

'You must remember to give me your financial details so that I can sort matters,' he said quietly.

Contempt blazed through the mask that Kate had so carefully constructed. She knew Francesco was clutching at straws, but she'd believed him above bribery. She turned and walked away.

'Kate . . . ?'

'What?'

'Goodnight, Kate. I hope you sleep well.'

'Oh . . . go to hell, Francesco!'

13

'I'm hungry, Mummy!' It was almost nine o'clock when Dominic came into her bed for a cuddle the next morning.

'I bet you are.' She hugged him tightly. 'Let's get you washed and see what we can find to eat. Haven't you had a good sleep!' It was a good sign, and so far he seemed back to normal.

She didn't much fancy the idea of bumping into Cesare and hoped that he breakfasted early, but when she opened her door she found a tray containing a jug of orange juice and some bread rolls and butter. Dominic fell on the rolls like a starved child, as indeed he was, but his abstinence had allowed his system to regain its balance.

'Let's go and find Uncle Francesco.' She held out her hand and he skipped beside her happily. One of the garden-ers pointed them in the direction of the swimming pool. Oh yes. She looked at the cloudless sky and felt the morning sun warming her body. If she lived here, that would be the first thing she'd do every morning.

Unaware of their presence, Francesco sliced through the water with incredible speed. Kate pursed her lips as she watched him. This was the man who'd challenged her to a race and pretended she'd won! Why on earth had he done that?

She started to laugh. Dominic had stripped down to his underpants and was tugging her arm.

'Yeah, go on,' she said, and he was in the water in no time. She sat on a sun lounger and watched him. When her son was in the water, most people did stop what they were doing and watch him. If they were being kind, they would remark that Dominic's style of swimming was enthusiastic. If they didn't like getting splashed, they were likely to say that he was a thorough nuisance and shouldn't be allowed in the baths. He was actually quite a strong swimmer, but more than one person had tried to rescue him because they thought he was in trouble. His arms and legs flailed wildly, and his sole purpose in swimming seemed to be to get as much water over the side of the pool as was in it.

As soon as Francesco saw his nephew, he flipped on to his side, bent his arm like a fin and started to chase him around the pool. As soon as they reached the shallow end, Dominic launched himself at Francesco, clung to his neck and was given a free ride for several lengths. Then he stood up and smiled at Dominic, who was still hanging from his neck. 'No more for the moment,' he said, before disentangling himself and striding out of the pool.

Dominic's mouth dropped open and she saw him formulating the words of protest then, to her utter amazement, he decided not to utter them. If she'd played with him like that and shook him off so peremptorily, he'd have pleaded with her for an hour to continue.

She watched the tall athletic figure of Francesco Mazzoni approach. Why had Dominic reacted so differently to him?

'*Buongiorno, Signorina*. I trust that you slept well.' His voice and manner were wary. After the manner in which she'd answered his goodnight the previous evening she couldn't altogether blame him.

'Very well, thank you.'

He picked up a towel and began to rub himself dry, which was rather a pity. The rivulets trickling down the half-naked torso, glistening in the early morning sunshine, could rate as a tourist attraction.

'I am pleased,' he said formally, then began to laugh as he caught sight of Dominic swimming. 'A style all of his own.' His eyes twinkled as they turned back to her. 'We shall have it included in instruction manuals from now on — The Dominic Mazzoni Style.'

'The Dominic Thompson Style,' she corrected quietly.

He appeared about to say something, but changed his mind. 'Quite,' he said, and rubbed his hair vigorously with the towel, before flinging himself on to the sun lounger beside her.

'Do you swim every morning?' she wanted to know.

'Not every morning. No.'

'And this morning?'

He frowned at her, not sure of her meaning. 'As you see.' He flicked an impatient hand across his body.

'It does present a tempting scenario, doesn't it?' She pointed to the pool where Dominic was splashing happily. 'You know how much I love swimming.'

'I don't believe this!' The wooden sun lounger clattered as Francesco sprang to his feet. 'Do you really think that I have been swimming up and down this pool since seven o'clock this morning, waiting for you to get up, in the hope of presenting an enticing scene so that you will stay here?'

Kate bit her lip. Put that way, no she didn't.

'Here. Look!' He thrust an arm near her face.

'At what?'

'The evidence, Kate. What happens to skin when it is immersed in water for any length of time?'

'All right, I believe you.' His arm was perfectly smooth without any trace of a water wrinkle.

'Thank you.' He checked his watch. 'I am sure that you are more aware of the timetable of flights to London than I am, so what time do you want to leave for the airport?'

She stared at him, incredulous. 'You'd take me? Just like that?'

He turned a dark face towards her. 'Kate, at this moment, I am inclined to take you whether you want to go or not.'

She hunched her knees up to her chin and rested her head on them. 'I'm sorry. I never said that I wasn't paranoid.'

He thought out loud. 'Double negative . . . yes, you are a little, Kate. I regret the circumstances that have made you so, but it is a little wearing.'

She could see how it could be. 'There's one thing I can't get my head around though.'

He sat back down and gestured with his hand that she should continue.

'Why was it so important to come here? You're in Britain often enough. I wouldn't have stopped you seeing Dominic every now and again.'

He frowned. 'You know why. For my father to meet him.'

'Yes, but at the beginning your dad didn't know anything about him. As soon as he did I expected pressure, but from him, not from you. Why was that, Francesco? Are you frightened of him?'

He gave a snort. 'Don't be ridiculous! Of course I'm not afraid of my father.'

'But plenty of people are, aren't they?'

He said nothing, but turned a speculative gaze on her.

'Nico told me that Cesare knew everyone of any importance in Rome. That, without a second thought, he would ruin a man for the smallest slight.'

Francesco ran a forefinger over the seat of the sun lounger. 'I am certain that Nico said a lot of things,' he said, not looking at her.

'So Nico was a liar?'

He sighed. 'Perhaps it was true. Once. But you have seen my father, Kate. He is an old man now.'

'Call me paranoid if you like, but you can see why I wasn't exactly in raptures about coming with you.'

For a second, anger flashed over his face, but Francesco's voice was calm as he answered. 'I assure you, Kate, that I have never adopted my father's methods of conducting business.' He paused, waiting for her to say that she believed him, but she'd have to know him a lot better before she could give him that assurance. People had accused her of not opening up to them, but she

235

was an amateur compared to Francesco. It was like getting blood out of a stone.

'You still haven't answered my original question,' she said finally.

'I haven't?' He seemed surprised, then got to his feet and strolled over to the pool house where he retrieved an inflatable dolphin and threw it into the swimming pool for Dominic to play with.

She sighed, sure that this was avoidance tactics and that when he returned he'd pretend to have forgotten the question.

'Parents,' he murmured, retaking his seat. 'You and I, we are similar perhaps?'

She looked at him in surprise. Nope, she didn't think so.

'I recall you mentioning last night that you owe a great debt to your mother and father. That as well as caring for you, they lent you the money for a secretarial course, which finally helped you to get out into the world and cope with Nico's death.'

'Yes.' She had absolutely no idea where this conversation was leading.

'I, too, am grateful for my father's help, for the assistance he gave me and for the risks he took in the early days when I often fell flat on my face and lost him a great deal of money.'

Mmm, well, not quite the same thing, but she could see from Francesco's face that he was sincere.

'Perhaps some children do feel this debt more than others.' He didn't say it, but Kate knew he was talking about his brother. Whatever Nico was given, it was never enough.

'I remember my father bristling with energy — a positive, vital man. Yes, it was always Nico that received the most attention, the most presents, but I accepted that.' He smiled and swept his hand airily. 'You know why.'

No, she didn't, but she wasn't going to risk asking him now and stem his flow. 'Go on,' she encouraged.

'After Nico died, I watched that man deteriorate into the person he is today.

Guilt, remorse, anger, frustration, all powerful emotions gnawing away at him. Help has been offered, but pride makes him refuse it. Perhaps it was wrong, but when I saw Dominic, the image of the child he had lost, I believed that meeting him would act as a catalyst. That it might help to reverse this degradation before it is too late. Forgive me, Kate, for landing you in the middle of it, but I still think it might.'

'I see.'

'So will you stay?'

'After what you've just told me, I've got to, haven't I?'

He smiled. 'Have you?'

'Of course, I have. And I'll tell you something else, Francesco. If you'd told me all this at the beginning you could have saved yourself an awful lot of aggro.'

He took both her hands in his and pressed them to his chest. 'Forgive me?'

'Yeah, all right.'

He hesitated. 'And the other?'

She pulled a face. 'I'm working on it.'

'Good enough.'

She pulled away and waved to Dominic that he should come out of the pool. With both her palms resting on the warm musculature of Francesco's chest and her stomach fluttering like a trapped moth, there was a danger that she might promise Francesco anything.

'It doesn't change anything,' she reminded Francesco, as he picked up a huge towel with which to wrap up her son.

'Hmm?'

'I might understand a bit more about your dad, but I still don't want to be in the same room as him.'

'You have it.'

★ ★ ★

'Happy?'

'Mmm.' They'd taken Dominic to the Villa Borghese Park, where they'd visited the zoo, travelled on the miniature railway and were at present

239

waving as he whizzed round and round in a giant ladybird on one of the children's rides.

As always, people assumed that they were married. The only clue that they weren't was the fact that they didn't walk hand-in-hand as other couples did, or that Francesco didn't put his arm around her. That aside, she couldn't have wished for a more attentive husband or Dominic for a more affectionate father. He never disagreed with anyone who thought that Dominic was his son and who pointed out their similarity of looks. Instead, he would smile and remark that Dominic was indeed a fine boy.

Francesco was good company. She'd probably need a tin-opener to make him reveal as much as he had that first morning, but on the surface he was bright, amusing, and practically a walking guidebook of information on the places they visited.

'It's almost over,' she said, voicing a regret that had been growing steadily for the past few days. It took her completely by surprise, however, that she'd actually said it.

'It doesn't have to be.' This time he did put his arm around her shoulder and hugged her to him momentarily. 'Stay for the summer, *car* . . . ' He stopped himself before uttering the forbidden word. 'Stay for the summer, Kate. You would be more than welcome.'

'And you'd continue to take us everywhere like you have this week?' She knew it was impossible, but wondered how he would answer.

He grimaced. 'Regretfully, no. But I would arrange matters so that I could spend as much time in Rome as possible.'

'I don't think so, but thanks anyway, Francesco. We've had a brilliant holiday. I appreciate it.' It was true. After that terrible first day, she'd relaxed and enjoyed the experience to the utmost. It was only marred when she inadvertently encountered Cesare in the villa.

241

Lord, how that man detested her! He nurtured and fed his hate until it was a brooding malevolent presence between them. It took almost an hour after any encounter before she recovered her equilibrium completely.

But Dominic sensed none of this. He went quite happily with Francesco to visit his other grandpa. She'd managed to stop him calling Cesare his 'smelly grandpa', which she thought was very noble of her. He came back afterwards bright and cheerful, and no matter how much she interrogated him, she could find no cause for concern.

Perhaps she should stay another week? As soon as she'd thought it, she dismissed it. The longer she stayed here, the harder it would be to get back to the real world. Seven days was quite enough to spend with the undivided attention of this man. He radiated charm the way a three-bar electric fire radiates heat. She knew it wasn't real, that he was attempting to atone for past sins, but it still made her stomach contract every time he turned that three-kilowatt smile on her. Mazzoni was as much out of her league as the future king of England. He knew that. She knew that. It was time to put some distance between them.

'I've things to do at home,' she said regretfully. Yep, minor little things like stopping the bailiffs coming in and pinching the furniture. 'We'll go the day after tomorrow, as arranged.'

He drew her to him and she gazed into the liquid darkness of his eyes. 'I shall miss you, Kate,' he breathed, and her stomach, that had been training all week for the Olympic swimming team, executed a perfect back-flip.

His face hovered above hers. She knew he meant to kiss her and she tilted her chin slightly to accommodate him. His full lips came closer; she felt his warm breath on her cheek and closed her eyes, then felt a tickling sensation on the tip of her nose. That was it? That was her kiss? Instead of the double back-flip that her stomach was poised to undertake, it splatted down in a belly flop.

Just what kind of kiss was a peck on the nose? It was the kind that she might give Dominic; it was a paternal type of kiss. Francesco was only a few years older, but was that how he viewed her — as a child? That she'd probably have kicked him if he *had* kissed her properly, didn't strike her as odd. Instead, she stared at his back, totally confused, as he went to retrieve Dominic from the ladybird.

'Do you want to go on anywhere else?' He turned back with a smile.

'No, I think that I've had enough.' In more ways than one, she told herself grimly. But the thought crossed her mind as to whether she'd still be thinking that way, next week, when the main excitement of the day would be the next episode of 'EastEnders'.

They returned to the car, Dominic hanging on to their hands and demanding to be swung up into the air every few minutes. His body bristled with life, and he'd spent the last few days on a peak of happiness. She sighed. It was going to be difficult for her to return to their everyday existence, but how much more difficult must it be for a six-year-old? An uncle had appeared, who took him on an aeroplane to a place where he could swim whenever he wanted, who drove him first in a Bentley and then in a Ferrari, and where the adults fell over themselves to cater for his every whim. How was she going to explain why this should suddenly cease, and why they had to queue for a bus whenever they visited his other grandpa.

'You're very quiet, Kate.'

She tore her gaze from the passing scenery and fastened it momentarily on Francesco. It puzzled her how he could drive so fast and still look so relaxed, and she usually was quiet when he drove for fear of distracting him. So he must have picked up on something else.

'Oh, you know.' She turned one of his favourite expressions back on him and saw from his compressed lips that he didn't like it any more than she did. She still wasn't certain whether he did think she knew more about him and his family than she did, or whether it was simply a ploy to stop her getting too close. She strongly suspected the latter.

'Have you given any more thought as to whether you wish to dine at the villa tonight or at the restaurant I told you about?'

Kate swivelled her head to check her son. He was staring dreamily out of the window. If he followed the pattern of previous days, he'd receive another burst of energy when they arrived back at the villa, use it up swimming, then afterwards have something to eat with Cesare. He'd fall asleep while she was reading to him, and sleep through until seven o'clock the next morning.

'I'd love to go out to dinner for a change,' she said.

'Excellent.' He turned his attention back to the road, and she closed her eyes while he overtook a lorry and

246

slotted into the tiny gap in front of it.

Dominic followed the pattern predicted for him. By six o'clock, he was zonked and didn't stir even when her elbow caught his table lamp and sent it crashing to the floor. She spent the extra time on face and body maintenance. The restaurant they were going to was so exclusive that, under normal circumstances, it probably wouldn't let her through the door as a waitress. The last thing she wanted, if she ended up in the Italian version of *Hello* magazine, was her mother chuntering on for evermore as to why she hadn't bothered with her make-up.

'You're looking pretty damn gorgeous, girl.' Kate checked her reflection in the mirror, puckered her lips and blew herself a kiss. Then she went out on to her balcony, poured herself a glass of wine and waited for Francesco.

Hadn't he said that they would leave at half-past-seven? She saw that it was now quarter-to-eight and wondered what he was doing? She could go downstairs and find out, of course, but she didn't want to risk running in to Cesare and spoiling the evening.

On cue, there was a knock at the door and Kate rushed to answer it. She greeted Francesco with a bright smile. She really was looking forward to this.

He stood there, immaculate in a dinner suit, but the tie hung loosely at his neck. 'You've forgotten to do your tie up.' She grabbed the two silken ends. 'Shall I have a go?'

His hands clasped around hers, stopping her. 'Forgive me, Kate, but we shan't be dining out this evening.'

Disappointment kicked her in the stomach and she pulled away from him.

'I am as disappointed as you,' he assured her.

'Don't worry about it. I'm sure that whatever it is, it's important.' She should have foreseen this. Whenever she'd been guilty of vanity in the past, something had come along to slap her right down again. 'So, can I invite you to dinner al fresco later?' She gestured to the balcony where they'd eaten most meals since she'd arrived.

He looked at the floor. 'I'm afraid not. I really need to sort out this problem tonight.'

'OK.' She tried to keep the flatness she felt out of her voice, but didn't succeed.

'I'll have something sent up, shall I?'

'Please.'

'Until tomorrow then.' He hesitated at the door, seemingly unwilling to leave. 'Kate . . . ?'

She looked at him.

'You look absolutely stunning.'

She looked down at the emerald green silk of her dress. 'Yeah, I know.' Pity that the only ones who were going to see it tonight were the mosquitoes out on the balcony.

Then he was gone.

She told herself that she was upset because she'd dressed up for nothing, because she'd missed out on visiting a restaurant that celebrities and super-models frequented, then she told herself that she was a liar.

She was upset because she was missing Francesco's company. For five days, she'd had his exclusive attention. Now, she felt like his girlfriends probably did when he grew bored and dumped them, despite the fact that all she'd received in the way of passion was a brief peck on the nose!

She wandered aimlessly around her room, unable to settle to anything. She saw now why he'd never married. He was an intense man whose boredom threshold was set to minimum. Whatever he did, he gave it his all, but when the task was completed he needed fresh stimulation. That explained the vast number of companies he owned. It also explained his behaviour towards Dominic.

That he was extremely fond of his nephew was in no doubt. When he was playing with him, there was a softness to his expression that she witnessed on no other occasion. But the end of play was always peremptory. He would snap a book closed, pack a game away, or heave himself out of the swimming pool, leaving her son howling for more.

Aware that there weren't many men who would play with a six-year-old for half as long, Kate told Dominic not to bother his Uncle Francesco, who then usually suggested that they play something different, like a game of football. So that was it — he wasn't bored with her son, just with the activity.

But pity the poor woman who tried to keep his attention for a lifetime! The magazines were littered with those who had been prepared to take on the challenge and failed. It would have been a lot easier for him if he could have been born a sultan and kept a harem.

Her dinner was delivered, and she sat in solitary splendour to eat it. So was Francesco really downstairs sorting out a problem or was five days his absolute limit of endurance to spend with one woman? Was the Ferrari at this moment hurtling along the autostrada towards a secret assignation and sexual excitement?

Kate let out a self-mocking cackle. Here was she thinking she was having dinner all by herself and she hadn't noticed Princess Paranoia joining her. Why should she care what Francesco got up to? The only reason she was here at all was because Fate had a warped sense of humour. If she hadn't given birth to his brother's child, she'd simply be another in a long line of secretaries whose name had slipped his memory.

She thought at first that it was a gunshot that startled her and caused her to cry out, but as the sky lit up with jagged forks of lightning she realised that it was thunder. If she'd been brave, she would have stayed outside and admired the show. As the heavens caught light, it was certainly as spectacular as any firework display. Instead, she scuttled inside, slammed the door, and closed the blinds.

Her heart could have powered a turbine as she climbed into Dominic's bed and cuddled him for comfort. Thankfully he didn't wake, so she didn't have to pretend that all was wonderful with the world when really she was scared out of her wits.

The storm raged all night, but Dominic woke up, ready to party, just after six o'clock.

'Please just play in your room for a little bit,' she pleaded. She'd crawled into her own bed some time around four o'clock. She felt hot, feverish, and had a thumping headache. She was in no fit state to assemble the Lego that her son was poking in her face.

Unfortunately, she really wasn't in a fit state to face anything that happened that day.

14

The telephone rang and with a groan, Kate rolled out of bed to answer it. She'd managed to blot out the clatter from the adjoining room, but the strident urgency of this machine was another matter.

'Yes?'

'Kate?'

'Last time I looked.' Who else did Francesco think it might be?

There was a pause. 'I'm going down to breakfast. I'd like you to join me.'

Kate stared at her watch. It was only five-to-seven. What was the big rush? 'I need a shower.' She sniffed the air. Yes, most definitely.

'I'll meet you downstairs in half an hour,' came the terse instructions before he hung up.

'And good morning to you too!' she muttered, replacing the receiver. She thought she was supposed to be on holiday.

It had gone quiet next door and, like all mothers, this worried her. She pushed open the door to investigate but, instead of Dominic trying to dismantle his wardrobe or some other forbidden activity, he was lying on the floor drawing. The surge of love that she felt for him at that moment shocked her. These moments always did. They came without warning and had an intensity about them that was almost debilitating.

'Aren't you a good boy! Oh, I do love you!' she said, and hugged him until he protested. Lord, he was so precious. He was her life.

'I'm going for a shower.' She stood up and smiled fondly down at him. His skin had turned a wonderful mocha shade, and he looked as if he'd lived here forever. 'Put your clothes on. Uncle Francesco's waiting for us.'

He was sitting on the terrace stirring a coffee moodily.

Kate stared at the dark circles under his eyes as she reached for a croissant. The shower had shifted her headache and, hopefully, once she'd eaten something she'd feel human again. 'You look a bit rough. Storm kept you awake as well, did it?'

He lifted his head. 'What storm?'

Her eyebrows shot up. 'That good, was she?'

'I have no idea what you are talking about,' he said wearily. 'Please eat your breakfast and then we're going out.'

'Are we?' Kate tried to remember what they'd planned for today, but as far as she recalled they'd discussed nothing.

Dominic was laboriously buttering a bread roll. 'Can I go for a swim first?'

Kate opened her mouth to say yes, but Francesco was quicker. 'No!' he snapped.

She glared at him. 'May I remind you that's my son you're talking to.'

Francesco glanced over at his nephew, who was staring at him wide-eyed. 'Sorry,' he murmured, and reached over to tousle his hair. 'Not this morning, Dominic.'

Kate poured herself a coffee. So, the honeymoon period of the ultra-nice, ultra-charming Francesco was collapsing. It had lasted a lot longer than she'd expected, and it would certainly make it a lot easier to leave.

'That black holdall that you sometimes bring out with you?'

Kate took a sip of coffee. 'What about it?'

'I want you to fill it with a change of clothes and anything you think you and Dominic might need for a couple of days.'

Kate stiffened. 'Why?'

'I'll explain later. And bring your passports as well.'

Her coffee spilled as she replaced the cup in its saucer. 'If this is a joke, Francesco, I swear I'll . . . '

'No joke.' He maintained a level gaze. 'If anyone asks, I'm merely taking you to throw a coin into the Trevi fountain. And just the one bag. Nothing different to usual.'

'I think that I'm going to be sick.' She pushed one half of her croissant away while the other heaved in her stomach.

'No, you're not.' He took her hand and squeezed it. 'You're going to walk calmly back to your room while Dominic finishes his breakfast.'

She looked at him wildly.

'Dominic will be fine,' he assured her, reading her thoughts. 'I won't go anywhere until you get back.'

Still she stared at him.

'You have to trust me, Kate. I'm doing this for you,' he said gently.

'You're scaring me, Francesco.'

'I'm sorry. I can't think of any other way.'

'Any other way of what?'

He sighed. 'Later. You're wasting time, Kate.'

She stood up, and although she wanted to tip her head back and scream until he told her what was going on, she managed to restrain herself. If anyone had stood close, they'd have heard the hammering of her heart trying to break out of its rib-cage. But nobody did. Nobody came near her as she walked unsteadily back to her room.

Francesco jumped to his feet as she returned. 'Try and keep it together, Kate.' Hysteria beckoned and she was teetering on its edge. 'It's going to be all right.' He rubbed briskly up and down her arms.

'It's not going to be all right!' She flashed him a look of intense hatred. 'Our passports are missing.'

A stream of invective flowed through his lips. He stopped, and raked a hand through his hair. 'All right, there is nothing we can do about it at the moment. Let us go.' He assessed her carefully. 'Will you make it to the car? Do you want a little more time?'

She gritted her teeth. 'I'll get there.' And feeling like an escaped criminal, she did. She flopped into the front passenger seat and allowed Francesco to strap Dominic into the back. The sun was warm on her face, but she was shivering as though it were mid-winter.

As Francesco put the car into gear and they moved away from the house, Kate closed her eyes and offered up thanks. She could only guess what was going on, but the further away from Cesare she was, the safer she felt.

They came to the wrought iron gates at the end of the drive. But the gates remained resolutely closed. Her panic, which she'd kept to a simmer, suddenly came to the boil and began to overflow. 'Oh God, oh God,' she muttered, hugging herself.

'Don't worry.' Francesco reached over to squeeze her arm before getting out of the car.

'Heavy night last night, Bruno? Are you asleep in there?' he shouted, walking over to the gatehouse. She saw him talking to a man inside and then, after a few moments, punch a number into his mobile phone and speak animatedly to the person on the other end. He then passed the phone to the gatekeeper, snatched it back and emerged into the sunlight, throwing insults over his shoulder to the person inside. He paused for a moment, winked at her, and continued.

A wink! Kate seethed. Her life was crumbling at the edges and he could wink! She couldn't look at him as he folded himself back into the Ferrari. She'd be tempted to do him serious damage. Then who would drive the getaway car?

The gates swung open and they shot through them in a cloud of dust. For once, Kate wasn't tempted to tell him to slow down as they hurtled down the hill. He couldn't drive fast enough for her. She saw him continually checking his rear-view mirror. Dear God, he was making sure that they weren't being followed. Was this a movie or was it her life? Whatever it was, they'd got the wrong person. She didn't want to be involved in a car chase around Rome. She wanted to be at home, spreading marmalade on her toast, moaning about the weather, and thinking what she needed at the shops.

He glanced solicitously at her from time-to-time, but she ignored him. Her control was barely holding and she knew that if she said one word to him, she'd lose it. She tightened her arms across her stomach and stared fixedly ahead. Francesco spoke instead to Dominic. She couldn't believe how calm he was. Someone had stolen their passports and they were trapped in this country, yet he could laugh and joke with her son as though they were going for a picnic.

'I hate you.' She couldn't prevent the words leaving her lips. They acted as a safety valve allowing some of the pentup emotion to escape. The first time she said it, he didn't seem certain whether he'd heard right, but he was under no such illusion the second and third time. His knuckles turned white as they gripped the leather steering wheel, and his banter with Dominic ceased.

They came to the resort of Bracciano, taking a side road that skirted the lake before halting at a large, shuttered house. While Francesco deactivated the alarm and opened the front door, Kate filled her lungs with fresh air and stared out over the water. Strange to look at something so beautiful and be completely unmoved.

'Are you hungry?' It was said in the tone of someone speaking to an invalid.

'No.'

'Dominic says he is. I'd like you to check these biscuits before I give them to him.'

Like an automaton, Kate did as she was bid. She watched Francesco settle her son in front of the Disney channel with biscuits, juice and an apple, and tried to prepare herself for what she knew was coming next.

'I want to talk to Mummy, Dominic,' he said. 'We'll be outside if you need us.' He closed the door and took her by the arm into the garden where he led her to a stone seat

263

overlooking the lake. Perfect for jumping into if what he told her proved too difficult to handle.

'My father informed me last night of his intention to take you to court to prove that you are an unfit mother,' Francesco began, then stopped as she struggled for breath.

She signalled for him to go on. If he didn't believe in beating around the bush then he might as well hit her with everything altogether.

'I'm sorry, there doesn't seem any way of softening this.'

'Spit it out!' she hissed.

'You were to be served with papers this afternoon, preventing you from leaving the country until the case . . . '

That was as far as he reached before she snapped, and it was all the more spectacular for having been held in for so long. Every word of abuse in English or Italian that she'd ever heard was dredged from her memory banks and spat at him. His face drained of colour, his body stiffened, and his fists clenched at his sides, but he didn't say a word until she'd finished.

'Thank you for sharing your feelings with me, Kate,' he said eventually. 'I take full responsibility for what has happened and I deserve everything you've said, but I hope that you've said it all. I wouldn't like to hear it again.'

Wouldn't he? The arrogance of the man! He'd just told her that she might lose her son and he was concerned about a few swear words! She opened her mouth to tell him so, but one look at the anger blazing beneath the surface stopped her. She'd been given one free shot but wouldn't be given another. It was as well that she'd taken full advantage of it.

'So what's the plan?' she hissed. 'Do we wait here, or do we just drive around until they catch us?'

A muscle twitched in his jaw. 'I'm taking you to a house that my father knows nothing about. I was unable to voice my objections too strongly last night, but I will once you are safe.'

Kate took a deep breath. It didn't really help. 'You invited me over here for a holiday, Francesco, not to sign up to a witness protection programme!'

He looked at the ground. 'I know, Kate. Believe me, I do know.'

She dropped her chin on to her hands, stared at the lake, and thought. Then she looked up at him. 'There are nuns with more active social lives than me. Even if I'm served with these papers, surely I don't have anything to worry about?'

His expression was unfathomable. 'You are being naïve, Kate,' he said.

'OK, spell it out.' She was on her feet now. 'Your father would bribe judges, witnesses, and do whatever it takes to get his own way — just like Nico said he would?'

He didn't answer.

'Why, Francesco? I brought Dominic to see him. I did what you asked.'

'I know.'

Kate studied his face. For better for worse, she was getting to know this man. He was hiding something.

'There's something you're not telling me,' she said.

15

'I have told you what my father plans to do,' he said.

'Yes, but not why.'

He turned away. 'It serves no purpose, Kate. Leave it.'

She grabbed his arm. 'Tell me, Francesco. I won't leave go until you do.'

He shook his head in resignation. 'You insulted my father in front of his staff.'

Kate was stunned. 'He insulted me first!'

'In private, Kate. In private.'

'Oh, and that's all right then, is it?'

He sighed. 'You asked me. I told you. It doesn't mean that I condone it.'

She couldn't believe it. 'So this is all my fault? If I hadn't shouted at him, none of this would have happened?'

He placed both his hands on her

shoulders to stop her pacing around. 'This is my fault, Kate, as you have so rightly pointed out. I shall put it right.'

'Tell me the truth, Francesco, do you really think that shouting at Cesare has caused all this?' Blue eyes scanned brown waiting for his answer.

He thought for a long time before answering. 'If I am perfectly honest, I believe that subconsciously he was searching for an excuse and you handed him one. He did not make a great deal of sense last night. I am sure that in a couple of days, he will see things differently.'

Kate wasn't convinced that he would, and she wasn't totally convinced that Francesco was telling her everything that he knew. So she listed her alternatives.

There were none.

Now she knew where she stood. She had no choice but to go along with Francesco, until she could think of something different.

'We should leave this place,' he said,

269

and began to walk back to the house.

Dominic was still immersed in the Disney channel. She picked up his cup and plate, washed them, and looked around for Francesco. She found him in the study, lifting down banknotes from a safe on the wall.

'Tell me that you do own this house, Francesco.'

He smiled for the first time that day. 'I do, yes.' He gestured to the notes. 'We shall not be able to use our credit cards for a while. They can be traced.'

She shrugged. 'They don't let me use mine anyway.'

As Francesco reset the alarm, Dominic bounded over to the Ferrari. 'I am sorry.' He looked at both his nephew and the car with regret. 'We will have to leave this behind.' He turned to her. 'My car will be the first thing that they will look for.'

She suppressed a shudder. She didn't like to think too closely about who 'they' might be.

He pointed his key ring at a garage, the door flipped open and he backed out a cream BMW before replacing it with the Ferrari. 'You've got a lot more room in the back of there,' she told Dominic, but he didn't look at all impressed.

They rejoined the autostrada and headed north towards Orvieto. 'Is it far?' she asked him.

'Once we reach Orvieto, I believe it should take us about an hour.'

Kate looked at him. 'You believe?' she said. 'Can't you remember?'

His shoulders lifted. 'I have never been there.'

She let out a snort of disbelief. 'What! You own a house that you've never even visited?'

His fingers gripped the wheel more tightly. 'That is what I said.'

She shook her head. 'That's immoral, Francesco. Half the world doesn't have enough to eat and you've got mansions littering half this country.'

He gave her a dark stare.

She folded her arms. 'OK, at this moment, I'm very glad that you've got a mansion tucked away that Cesare knows nothing about.'

His lips curved slightly. 'Hardly a mansion, I would imagine.'

'And it's hardly likely to be a hut, I would imagine,' she countered.

'For all I know it might be.' He seemed to be enjoying this game while she was becoming more and more irritated.

He sighed when he saw the expression on her face. 'A friend of mine was in financial difficulties. I took the house from him in exchange for repayment of a debt.'

Kate digested this information. 'Did he have anywhere else to live?' she asked, and received such a scathing look in return that she assumed the answer to be yes.

Half an hour after they'd left Orvieto, Francesco halted outside a small grocery store. 'It may be prudent to stock up on supplies here.' He got out of the car, lifted his arms to the sky and stretched lazily.

'Whatever you think we might need.' He handed her a basket.

'Will there be anything there at all?'

'I have no idea.'

'This might take some time,' she muttered, throwing soap, washing-up liquid, and toilet cleaner into the basket, while he swanned to the front of the shop and called on the owner to slice her finest cheeses and ham for him.

She filled one basket, placed it on the counter and reached for another. 'This place will have a fridge, won't it?' she asked, eyeing the dairy counter.

'I would imagine so.'

Another thought struck her and she grabbed some candles and a box of matches. 'And electricity?' Were they going to arrive there and find everything cut off?

He smiled.

'Don't tell me, Francesco. You would imagine so . . . ?'

Again he smiled. 'I can tell you for certain that we have electricity. Giulio used the house as a fishing retreat. I intended to do the same and have been paying the bills.'

As Francesco loaded the groceries into the boot, Kate went through the list of items in her head. Had they forgotten anything? 'Sheets? Duvets?' she asked, as Francesco slammed the boot closed.

He nodded. 'I expect so.'

Kate wasn't so certain. 'Are you sure, Francesco? If this Giulio used to take his mates with him, the most we're likely to find is a pile of smelly sleeping bags.'

She couldn't understand why her comment amused him so much.

'Forgive me, Kate.' He raised his hand in apology. 'The only 'mate' Giulio used to take with him, was his mistress. Try as I might, I cannot imagine her rolling about in a sleeping bag — smelly or otherwise.'

'Who said anything about rolling

about?' she said and got back into the car.

As they turned off on to a road that wasn't marked on the map she was following, Kate was grateful that they'd bought so much food. For the last fifteen minutes, she'd seen no trace that humans actually existed in these parts and, as she looked out at the savage wilderness, she could understand why. The only sound was that of the curses Francesco was muttering under his breath as he swerved to avoid the rocks and potholes that were strewn liberally in their path. In fact, she wondered if they were on the right road, but decided it would be prudent not to enquire.

Yep, the man was lost. If they continued along this track, they were going to drive slap bang into a mountain. As far as she could see, and she had pretty good eyesight, there was absolutely no way around it.

Then they turned a corner and she saw the house and the river behind it, fed by a waterfall sparkling down the mountain. 'Oh wow!' She jumped out of the car as soon as it stopped, then caught Dominic as he ran past.

'Don't you dare go down there on your own.' She pointed to the fast flowing river. He nodded, but she saw that his mind was too full of present novelties. She'd repeat it at ten-minute intervals until it sunk in.

'I must check the spare before we attempt that again,' muttered Francesco.

'Your mate Giulio must have brought his mistress here by helicopter,' she joked.

He surveyed the area critically. 'It is possible.'

Slowly, Kate shook her head. With this man anything was possible. 'Let's have a look at the house then,' she said, walking towards the whitewashed stone building that had originally started life as a shepherd's hut. 'I don't suppose there's much of a vandal problem around here.' She tried to imagine what state the building would be in if it was left empty in London!

There were no alarms to deactivate. Francesco inserted a key into the lock and pushed the door open. Kate followed him and sniffed a slight mustiness. Nothing that opening the windows wouldn't clear. They walked straight into the living room, tiny, but with better furnishings than she had at home. She breathed a sigh of relief — she hadn't known what to expect. She walked straight through to the kitchen and felt like a fifties housewife as she saw a fridge. The wonders of modern science! How had they managed without it?

'I've seen the room I want.' Dominic tugged at her arm for her to come and look.

'Just a second.' She opened the fridge. A bit iced up, but it seemed to be working all right. 'OK. Lead on.' She smiled at her son, who immediately pulled her upstairs.

They met Francesco on the landing.

He was investigating a cupboard and pointed out the sheets and blankets inside.

'Great.' She smiled at him too.

There were three bedrooms. Dominic wanted the smallest one, which was fortunate because the bed in it was only designed for a child. There was a double one, which Francesco could have. She didn't fancy lying in that bed imagining Giulio and his mistress rolling around in it. And there was another small one, with room only for a single bed, but at least it was a full-size one.

'Do you think this will suit?' Francesco looked doubtful.

'It's fine.'

'Is it?' His face cleared.

There didn't seem to be a bathroom. She ran downstairs and found a small one behind a door in the passage leading from the kitchen. It contained the basics. 'Yep, it's fine,' she shouted back upstairs.

And at least sorting out their living

conditions and trying to amuse Dominic without recourse to his toys would help to divert her mind from other matters. Could the fear that she'd lived with since Dominic was born materialise? Could the Mazzonis really snatch her son?

Francesco tramped downstairs, holding Dominic's hand as they walked to the car. Having one of them on her side helped, but all she could hope was that Francesco was cleverer or, she shuddered at the thought, played dirtier than his father.

They returned with some of the groceries. As Francesco laid a cardboard box on the table, she half-expected him to look around with a quizzical expression for the servant who was meant to unpack it. But he didn't. He transferred butter, cheese, milk and other foodstuffs from the box to the fridge as though he unloaded the shopping every day. She left them to it and went upstairs to make the beds.

'You should have called.' Francesco

walked in while she was struggling with the sheet for the double bed. He calmly took the opposite end, pulled it tight, and tucked it in.

'Did you have to do household chores in exchange for pocket money when you were little?' She wondered if something in their upbringing could possibly be the same.

He laughed. 'No.'

'Where's Dominic? She hurried out to the landing.

'He is safe.' He followed her and pulled blankets from the cupboard.

'That river terrifies me.' She pointed out of the window.

'I have warned him not to go near it without me.' He shook the top sheet into the air and settled it over the bed. 'But we can see everything from here. He wouldn't get very far.'

'So what's he doing?'

'He has found a trowel in the garden and is at present transplanting the pot of basil that we bought into a hole.'

'Why?'

He grinned. 'I thought you might know the answer to that.'

He went downstairs when they had finished the bed, while she took another blanket into Dominic's room in case he was cold during the night. Then she looked in each of the rooms to check that everything was in order. Strange. Apart from her dad, that was the first time she'd made a bed with a man. She gazed at the white cotton coverlet neat against the polished mahogany frame. It looked inviting. Lord, wouldn't it be wonderful right now to be able to blot out everything and lie there, crushed in Francesco's arms.

Kate shook herself. Where in the hell had *that* thought come from? She hurried downstairs before there were any more. She found Francesco sitting on the doorstep watching Dominic fill plant pots with soil.

'What's going to happen now, Francesco?' she asked, unable to hold it in any longer.

He looked up and lifted his arm in

silent invitation that she should sit beside him but, conscious of the thoughts she'd just had in his bedroom, she leaned against the door frame instead. 'Do you think your dad is going to drop everything just because you oppose him?'

He twisted round so that he was leaning against the opposite frame and so that he could see her more easily. 'It is probable. If he alienates me then he will have no one, and his dream of a dynasty founded by him and carried forward by his sons will have crumbled to dust.'

Kate mused over his words. 'It is probable', he'd said when the word she'd hoped to hear was 'yes'.

There was a catch in her voice as she voiced her fear, 'And if he takes no notice?'

'Then we switch to plan B.' Francesco smiled at her.

'Which is . . . ?'

'Which is what I'll have to think about if the occasion arises.'

'Oh God.' Kate wrapped her arms around herself and walked away.

He was beside her instantly. 'Don't worry, Kate. I am not going to let my father take Dominic. I promise you.'

'Don't worry,' she murmured. Why did people always tell her that? It was one of the few things that she was good at. Hell — she practically had a degree in it! But maybe she should leave it until she had something concrete to worry about. Where was the satisfaction with this half-hearted worrying when, in a couple of days, she might be able to overdose on the real thing.

'Right,' she said, determined to pretend that that argument had convinced her. 'I better think about making something. We've barely eaten all day.'

'A light lunch of bread and cheese, I think,' he stated authoritatively. 'Dinner this evening is on me.'

'Oh?' Kate glared at him. She wasn't at all keen on being told what food they should eat. 'The pizza delivery van can make it down here all right, can he?'

His head shot up as he took in the tone of her voice, then he started to laugh. 'Your brand of sarcasm is truly vicious, Kate. Have you always had the talent or have you had to work on it?'

Chastened by his good humour, Kate felt herself flush. 'Sorry,' she mumbled. 'I've upset a lot of people in my time.'

With a smile quivering on his lips, he remained watching her until she retreated into the kitchen. She opened the fridge, resisted the urge to bring out some cooked meat and brought out the cheese instead. She didn't hear him come in, and when she turned round and bumped into his muscular frame she let out a cry.

'Such an intriguing mixture of hardness and softness.' With the side of his hand he brushed down her cheek. 'Quite an enigma.'

She backed away and picked up the knife to cut the bread. 'You shouldn't go creeping up on people when they've got a knife in their hand,' she said, brandishing it at him.

He grinned. 'I rest my case.'

Kate applied herself to cutting up the bread. She fervently hoped that he was simply winding her up in order to get his own back, and that making the bed with her hadn't put the same ideas into his mind, as it had in hers.

Her unique brand of sarcasm might amuse him. A knee to the nether regions might not!

16

Returning from a walk to the river, Kate put the kettle on and turned to Francesco. 'Are you really making dinner tonight?' If not, she was going to start; she was getting hungry.

'Yes, we are.' Francesco winked at Dominic, who started to bounce up and down. 'I am going to teach my nephew how to prepare *penne alla primavera* so that he can impress his girlfriends when he is older.'

She gave her son a big hug. 'I'm impressed already.'

She left them to it and took her coffee into the living room. What should she do? There was no television, no radio, no nothing. She looked around to see if there were any books, then remembered she'd seen one on the floor of the car when she'd unfastened Dominic's seat belt. Please let it be one she hadn't read. There was nothing else here.

Francesco's keys were lying on the table. She picked them up and went hunting. Yes, a nice fat paperback wedged under the seat. She scanned the author and title, a lovely frothy bonk-buster she could lose herself in. Then she frowned. What was it doing in Francesco's car?

She walked into the kitchen. Francesco had poured boiling water over some plum tomatoes and was showing Dominic how to take the skins off.

'Look what I found in your car!'

He glanced at the book. 'Good for you.'

'Doesn't look like your type of book.'

He looked more closely. 'It isn't mine.'

'Whose is it?' she asked, wondering if he would tell her, but quite accepting that his next words would be to mind her own business.

They weren't. He frowned at the

cover of the book and, fascinated, she watched the process between puzzlement and enlightenment play out over his features. The tiniest quirk of a smile marked the moment of recognition of the book's owner. 'I can't recall,' he said, handing the book back.

'Liar.' She snatched it from him and walked out of the room.

But she couldn't settle to reading. The two people in the other room seemed to be having much more fun, and she began to feel excluded. She wandered back. Francesco smiled and handed her a glass of wine, and she perched on the work surface to watch what they were doing. Francesco was chopping onions like a professional and shouting out words to Dominic, who was attempting to spell them with the pasta shells he'd tipped over the table.

'I've never been able to do that.' She pointed to the onions.

'The secret is in the wrists.' He demonstrated the action. 'Come here and I'll show you.'

She made a half-hearted attempt. 'No. I think I'll stick to my own method. I'm going to chop my finger off.'

He clicked his tongue in disgust. 'I'm disappointed in you. Even Dominic can do it.'

'Francesco!' She whirled round to give him a piece of her mind, but he was laughing.

'I thought I'd make you happy,' he said.

'And how's that supposed to make me happy?'

He grinned, and she realised that she'd just swallowed the bait he'd offered. As he knew she would. He tipped the onions into a frying pan and turned back to her with a shrug. 'It always seems to make you happy when you're thinking the worst of me.'

'That's not true.' Her response was automatic, but she filed his comment away to pick at later.

With one hand, he stirred the onions

as they sizzled and filled the kitchen with a delicious aroma and, with the other, he poured himself a tumbler of wine, took a gulp and threw the rest into the pan. 'Where's my helper?' he demanded.

Dominic left what he was doing and immediately stood up. Almost to attention, like a little soldier, she thought.

'Show mama how well you've chopped the tomatoes,' he ordered, and Dominic obeyed.

She peered into the bowl. 'How did you chop these?' she asked. She couldn't help herself.

She couldn't distinguish what Francesco said from the other side of the room. Perhaps it was as well.

Dominic showed her the pair of scissors he'd used before taking the bowl over to Francesco. 'Right, young man.' He lifted Dominic on to a cardboard box so that he could look into the pan. 'See how the garlic and onions have started to turn brown and there's hardly any liquid left in there?'

Dominic nodded energetically.

'Now is the time to add the tomatoes.' He smiled at his nephew. 'Your job.'

With a grin, Dominic sloshed the tomatoes into the mixture. Unfortunately, he was so eager that half of them sloshed right back out again and Francesco, who was crouched down ready for any mishap, received most of them.

Kate let out a cackle and began to laugh so hard that she almost fell off the work surface. Dominic looked from her to his uncle, uncertain of his position, then his instincts took over and he burst out laughing.

Francesco grabbed a tea towel to wipe his face. 'Didn't I tell you how happy it would make mummy if we did the cooking, Dominic?' he said with a wry grin.

Kate ran a finger under her eyes to brush away the tears. 'I've heard people say how much fun they had in the days before television. I never believed them until now.'

'I need to change my shirt.' He threw the tea towel to one side. 'Keep an eye on this pan, would you?'

'Is Uncle Francesco cross?' Dominic whispered when he'd gone.

Kate grinned and shook her head. 'No, he's not.' Surprisingly.

'Another job.' Francesco handed Dominic a bowl and the pair of scissors when he returned. 'I want you to cut some leaves off your basil plant and snip them as small as you can into here.' As soon as he'd run off, he opened a tin of tomatoes and poured them into the pan.

'Isn't that cheating?' she asked.

He nodded. 'Yes, but I'd quite like to eat sometime before midnight.'

'I'm sorry for laughing at you; it wasn't personal.'

'I didn't take it personally. I have a feeling that even if a head of state or some other distinguished personage had been standing there, that laugh of yours would still have rang around the kitchen.'

She pulled a face. 'Yeah, it's not my most attractive feature, is it?'

'Melodious as the tinkling of tiny bells.'

She demonstrated another cackle. 'As sarcasm goes, Francesco, that's pretty pathetic.'

He turned to give the pan a stir. 'It lacks the killer instinct, I do agree.'

Dominic ran back and handed his bowl to Francesco, whose quickly concealed look of dismay convinced Kate that cooking with children hadn't been quite the breeze he'd anticipated. Still, she had to give him top marks for perseverance. 'You're doing all the work, Dominic. Do you want to grate the cheese or shall I do that?'

While he handed her son a slab of cheese and a grater, Kate grabbed the bowl and picked out bits of soil, pieces of stick and pieces of anything that shouldn't be in it.

The end result was better than she

expected. She wondered if it really was so good, or was it that Francesco seemed to follow her own ploy when entertaining — make sure your guests are sufficiently lubricated and they'll believe anything tastes wonderful.

After lauding them both with praises, she took Dominic up to bed. She had intended to come back downstairs but, on passing her room, her bed looked so inviting that she crawled into it and knew nothing else until morning.

Sunlight streaming through her window woke her. She checked her watch — just after eight. Then she checked for noises; there were none. It would be a miracle if Dominic was still asleep. She got out of bed to look, but as she pulled back the curtains she saw them both by the river. They appeared to be fishing.

The kitchen smelled of fresh detergent. Everything had been washed, dried and put away, and the surfaces were gleaming. Kate put the kettle on and looked around guiltily. She'd make sure she did her share today. While the coffee was brewing, she washed and dressed, then made a drink for Dominic and carried them down to the river.

'*Buongiorno, mamma*,' said Dominic, and giggled. Francesco was teaching him phrases, but he was still self-conscious about using them.

'*Buongiorno, bambino*,' she answered, and kissed him.

She put a coffee beside Francesco, who wedged his rod between two rocks and stretched lazily before picking it up.

'Thanks for clearing everything up.' She smiled at him. 'Caught anything yet?'

He shook his head.

'Good.'

'Good?' He looked at her.

'It's my turn to cook tonight and there's no way I could mess about with those slimy things. I've rang up, and the pizza man's setting off now.'

His lips curved. 'I don't mind cooking. It's rare to have the opportunity.'

'So how come you're so good? Did you go to classes?'

'No.' He seemed to find this amusing. 'My father taught me.'

'Cesare?' To say she was gobsmacked was an under-statement.

He looked at her quizzically. 'That is the only one I have.'

She lapsed into silence and sipped her coffee. 'Are you going to get in touch with him today?' she asked eventually.

He stood up and threw the dregs of his coffee on to the grass. 'That is what he will expect me to do, therefore I will contact him tomorrow.'

Kate wondered whether annoying Cesare was really the best course of action, but Francesco knew his father better than she did. She had no choice but to trust his judgement.

'I suppose I'd better ring my parents.' Kate stood up.

'I thought you did it yesterday.'

She pulled a face. 'No, I put it off. I couldn't think what to say and I don't want to upset them.'

'What have you decided to say?'

She took a deep breath. 'That I'm having such a good time that I've decided to stay another week and can they check the flat and water the plants.'

He nodded. 'I think that is for the best.'

'Yes.' She twisted his meaning. 'I wouldn't like my poor little spider plant to snuff it.' She held out her hand to Dominic. 'Do you want to come back with me?'

His hands gripped the rod and his little body went rigid. 'Do I have to?'

'Not if you don't want to,' she said, and saw him relax. As she walked away, she felt a stab of emotion. Dominic had always been like her shadow, but he hadn't even looked up when she'd said goodbye. Her baby was growing up fast.

They were still there at twelve o'clock so she took them some lunch. 'Don't feel that you have to look after him all the time,' she whispered to Francesco.

He shook his head. 'Your son is excellent company. I am enjoying myself enormously.'

Kate picked up a stone and threw it into the river. Had Francesco lost sight of the reason why they were in this place? He was acting as if he were on holiday! She picked up another stone and threw it further. For now, she'd keep her misgivings to herself. His good humour might be a good omen: if he didn't seem worried about what might happen tomorrow, then perhaps she needn't be either.

She heard a deep voice behind her. 'We've been doing it wrong, Dominic,' it said. 'Mama is showing us how. We're not supposed to catch the fish, we're supposed to hit them on their heads.'

It amused her son. She smiled as his laughter rang out over the water, and turned to Francesco. 'Sarcasm's definitely improving.'

He gave a slight bow. 'Practice,' he murmured.

She kicked at the stones under her feet. 'If you won't let me brain any more fish, I'll go back.'

He came over to her and waited until she looked up at him. 'You're very welcome to stay,' he said softly.

'No. I need to wash some clothes.' She walked away, then turned back. Dominic was concentrating on his fishing and wasn't watching her. But Francesco was.

★ ★ ★

There might have been a power cut, and they might have been forced to eat their dinner by candlelight, but there was still electricity in the house. It crackled between them with each word or gesture that Francesco made. The house was too small for his presence, especially when Dominic wasn't there to deflect his attention. Her exhausted son had been tucked up in bed for hours.

Francesco propped his chin on his

hand and gazed across the table. 'Your skin has the most amazing glow in this candlelight.'

Kate's heart fluttered strangely. Normally she could treat his compliments as the insincere statements they were and allow them to bounce off her. Tonight, however, she found it more difficult. They came equipped with tiny barbs that clung to her and wouldn't be shaken off.

'It's almost translucent,' he continued.

She stood up. 'I'm going to wash up.'

His chuckle sent ripples over her stomach. 'In the dark?' he enquired silkily.

She grabbed one of the candles. 'If I put this on the window ledge, I'll be able to see.'

He was behind her, his breath stirring her hair. 'Leave it, Kate, I'll do these in the morning.'

'No, it's OK, it won't take long.' She put the candle in a glass. 'Go and sit down.' Please go and sit down. She didn't like this game. She didn't want to play.

'So soft.' He ran the tips of his fingers gently down her arms.

'OK, I'll leave them.' She turned to escape but couldn't. Behind her the rim of the sink pressed into her back, and in front stood the equally immovable presence of Francesco. Trapped between a sink and a hard place came the thought, but it didn't make her laugh.

'Good idea.' Francesco stepped closer, and the whole world shrank to the few feet that their bodies encompassed.

'Francesco, I . . . ' she began, but the rest of her words were lost as he bent to kiss her. His lips were warm and sensual, their touch the merest pressure on her own, not at all the violent plundering she'd imagined would be his style.

She began to relax as the kiss remained gentle, non-threatening. And, like someone on a perpetual diet unexpectedly offered a chocolate gateau, she decided that just a little bit wouldn't hurt. What was the harm in a little kiss?

Silken fingers trailed down her back, seeking out the sensitive places that sent delicious tremors coursing through her body. Gently, very gently the pressure increased as he eased her towards him. She knew that she should stop this. But, oh God — it felt so good!

Instead, she coiled her arms around his neck and moulded her body to his. She gasped as she encountered the evidence of his arousal, but as she opened her lips he slid his tongue smoothly between them. This was cheating. She should stop him.

But as the warm velvet texture brushed against her own, she began to quiver with anticipation. His tongue met no resistance as it explored the sweet hidden recesses of her mouth, and neither did his lips as they pulled away to explore the tender flesh of her neck, in their search for the tiny erogenous zone a few centimetres below her ear that would overload her senses.

He was close. Her nerve ends tingled and she felt herself beginning to drift, losing all conception of anything bar the sensations flooding through her.

If only they'd had longer. If only they'd been allowed to follow their natural inclinations that night. It might have been so much easier later.

But Fate, with its warped sense of humour, couldn't resist the opportunity for a good laugh.

17

The shock of it made her cry out, catapulting her from the haven she'd slipped into where only feeling and sensation were important.

The power cut was over, and the overhead light in the kitchen held her in its beam like a searchlight.

She stared at Francesco, aghast. What on earth had she been thinking of?

He returned the stare, his eyes mocking, his body taunting her as it remained welded against her own.

'Please, Francesco.' She pressed against his chest, but it would take greater strength than she possessed to move him if he chose not to.

His full lips formed a sardonic bow. 'Please what, Kate? Please take me upstairs to finish what we started?'

Arrogant man! He knew exactly what she meant. 'We didn't start anything,' she said, but wasn't surprised at the laughter that vibrated through his chest.

'You could have fooled me.'

'Nothing happened,' she said, and thanked God for allowing her to see the light literally and metaphorically in time.

He made no attempt to move away from her. 'Nothing more than usually happens when two people are physically attracted to each other,' he drawled.

It might happen to him all the time, but it certainly had never happened to her. Even with Nico, she'd followed the usual courtship rituals. That his brother inferred that she'd be an easy lay incensed her, and that he was so very nearly proved right made it worse.

'Get away from me, Francesco,' she said.

He moved back so that they weren't touching, but not enough that she could escape. 'Tell me what has changed in the last few minutes?' he demanded. 'You can't tell me that you weren't enjoying what we were doing.'

She glared at him. No, she couldn't tell him that. That would be insulting his intelligence. 'It was a mistake.'

'In what way?'

He couldn't leave it, could he? He couldn't take no for an answer. He had to persist until she blurted out anything that might explain the irrationality of her behaviour. Even if it wasn't true.

'I forgot it was you,' she said, and his head moved back with as much force as if she'd delivered a blow.

He remained there for several more moments, gazing at her, waiting for something.

Was it an apology? It crossed her mind to offer one until she remembered how easily he'd expected her to go to bed with him, and she decided to keep quiet. As it stood, there was no way that he'd ever be tempted to kiss her again, and that suited her. Her feelings towards him were too complicated. At this moment, her life was too complicated. She couldn't afford to be just another notch on Francesco Mazzoni's bedpost.

But she couldn't stand this laser-stare interrogation. Slowly, she turned and reached for the hot water tap to fill the washing-up bowl. The temperature in the kitchen dropped several degrees at the force of the icy blast that emanated from him. And with a wrench that nearly pulled the back door off its hinges, he opened it and stormed outside.

Kate turned off the tap, warmed her hands in the water for a few seconds, then tipped it down the sink. She would wash the dishes in the morning. She freely admitted that she was a coward, but she didn't think that there would be many people who would want to be still standing in that kitchen when Franceso returned.

★　★　★

He was usually an early riser, but there was no sign of him the following morning. She hadn't heard him come to bed the previous night and, with her heart hammering in her chest, Kate opened the door to check that his car was still there. Could she have upset him so much that he would just pick up his car keys and leave them to it?

The beige BMW glinted in the early morning sun, and she was so pleased to see it that she blew it a kiss. She closed the door quietly and went to make her and Dominic's breakfast.

At ten o'clock, he still hadn't appeared. An empty whisky bottle at the side of the sofa in the living room hinted why. She plucked up her courage and took him a cup of coffee.

He groaned, holding his head in his hands as he sat up and twisted out of bed. Kate, who thought he was naked, averted her eyes.

'I am decent,' came the acerbic tones, and she looked back again to discover that he was wearing a pair of black boxer shorts. Her gaze lingered over his muscular torso. Was this the man whose advances she'd so cuttingly refused last night? She must have been out of her mind!

She pushed the thought to the back of her brain where it belonged. 'The bread's rock hard, but there's some biscuits and cake if you fancy them.'

'Coffee's fine.' He sipped the coffee, but closed his eyes as though it was too much effort to keep them open.

'I think I've got a couple of aspirins in my handbag,' she said, taking pity on him.

'Thank you.'

When she returned with them and a glass of water, he was still sitting on the edge of the bed but he'd pulled on a polo shirt and a pair of jeans. Kate felt it as a rebuke — if she'd had no intention of sampling his wares, then she definitely had no right to be ogling them.

'I wish last night had never happened,' she said.

He didn't look at her. 'You made that perfectly clear last night.'

'I didn't mean that,' she began, but he put up a hand to stop her.

'Leave it, Kate. My head aches with trying to understand you. I don't wish to start a new day by beginning all over again.'

'I don't think that's what's making your head ache,' she said, but she was leaving as she said it. She closed the door and rested her head momentarily against it. Lord, why did she always need to have the last word? What made her provoke him like this? She must have a death wish!

He came downstairs five minutes later, smiled warmly at Dominic and praised the picture he was drawing, but only speaking to her with icy politeness. They went for a walk together shortly afterwards and Kate watched them from the upstairs window. Yes, his manner towards his nephew was as affectionate as ever, for which she was truly grateful. Dominic had begun to idolise Francesco and didn't deserve that his hero should suddenly turn cold on him because of her stupidity.

And she was stupid. She couldn't quite believe how much. Of all the days she had to pick to alienate this man, it had to be the day when she needed him the most. He hadn't said a word yet about phoning his father. Perhaps when he came back, he would announce that he'd decided not to bother.

She'd been good. With Francesco on her side telling her that everything was going to work out all right, she'd managed to put her worries on hold until events proved otherwise. Now, however, there was nothing to stop her brooding over what might go wrong. She made the beds, tidied Dominic's room, and went downstairs to indulge herself to the limit.

Dominic hurtled into the room brandishing a fossil that they'd found. She admired it, then wondered if he might find any more in the garden.

'What on earth is the matter?' asked Francesco when her son had gone to look.

Kate inspected her fingers that an hour before had fingernails on the end of them. 'Guess,' she said in a small voice.

'Tell me that you haven't been sitting there worrying that I'm not going to keep my promise to you?' he demanded.

Her head jerked up as she registered his anger, but she couldn't deny the truth. It was undoubtedly written all over her. She shrugged her shoulders in acknowledgement.

His hands clenched into fists at his side. 'Do you have any conception of how insulting that is? Do you really think so little of me that you imagine me capable of breaking my word because of what passed between us last night?'

'Sorry,' she said. He was blazing mad. Last night was simply a practice run.

'You're sorry? I'm sorry, Kate. I thought we were beginning to develop some kind of understanding between us, you and I, but I see that I am totally mistaken. I'm sorry for the wrong I did to you in the past. I'm sorry for bringing you to Italy against your will. Believe me — I'm even sorrier that I *ever* hired you as my secretary!'

He grabbed the telephone from the side table and punched in some numbers. 'And now I am going to phone my father. As I always intended to.'

'Shouldn't . . . ' She was about to suggest that he calmed down first. But the look he gave her shrivelled the words at source.

'I'll leave you to it.' She shot out of the chair and went to find Dominic.

It seemed like hours later before Francesco appeared in the garden. She took a deep breath and prepared herself for the worst, but he strode straight past her towards the river. Dominic ran after him but was summarily dismissed back to her care.

'*Oh, no!*' Heedless of the white dress she was wearing, Kate sat on a mound of soil and buried her head in her hands. She might not be the most perceptive person around — but something told her that this was definitely *not* a good sign.

18

He wasn't at the river long. He glanced at her as he walked past. 'I have phone calls to make before we can discuss this.'

Kate watched him as he strode back to the house. The anger had left his body and the aura of positive confidence that normally emanated from him had returned. He didn't appear at all dejected. So why did she? She picked up a stick and trailed it in the dirt. Let this be over soon. All she wanted now was to know her Fate.

It wasn't over soon. She went in to make lunch and she could still hear the steady drone of his voice from the living room.

He came out as they were finishing eating, and one look at the fixed expression on his face made Kate glad that she'd forced some food down her before she heard his news. She certainly didn't think she'd have managed after.

He crouched down in front of Dominic. 'I'm sorry that I have not been much fun this morning, young man. Will you be patient with me a little longer? I need to speak to Mummy, and then I promise you that I will make the swing that we were discussing yester-day.'

Dominic nodded solemnly. Even he had seemed to pick up on the gravity of the situation.

'In the meantime, perhaps you could go to your room and draw me a picture of my Ferrari? I'm beginning to forget what it looks like.'

With Dominic gone, he held out his hand to her. 'Come and sit on the seat. It's more shaded there. Your shoulders are burning.'

Kate shrugged. Peeling shoulders were the least of her problems. But his hand remained, so she took it.

'My father intends to go ahead with his plan,' he informed her the moment she sat down. It was what she expected him to say, but it still left her gasping for breath.

'I have contacted my lawyer and instructed him to do whatever it takes to fight this.' He sighed. 'My father is aware of my determination, but will not be dissuaded at this time from continuing this ridiculous course of action.'

'At this time?' She grasped at the only positive words in his speech. 'So is he likely to in the future?'

He grimaced. 'If I were a betting man, I do not think I would be laying my money down quite yet.'

'Great.' She knew that he was waiting for her to react, begin screaming or kicking at him. His body was tensed ready. But she hadn't the energy. She felt curiously flat, like a punch bag emptied of all stuffing.

'I won't lie to you, Kate, this is going to be extremely bloody.' He continued almost to himself, 'If my father does not back down, his action will publicly tear this family apart. I will not speak to him again, my mother will finally divorce him, and I will sell every share in every company in which he and I are associated.'

'No!' Caught up in her own part in this drama, Kate had given little thought to Francesco's.

'The media will have a feast,' he murmured, before crouching down in front of her and gripping her hands.

Kate looked at him in surprise. Now he was treating her like he did Dominic.

'They will print lies about you, Kate. I will protect you as much as I am able, but they will hurt. Unfortunately, they will be my father's lies — so there is nothing I can do about them until the case is concluded.'

Kate felt tears prick her eyes. Oh dear God, her parents! Her dad! What was all this going to do to him? Through a misty blur, she gazed up at Francesco.

'There has to be a compromise,' she pleaded. 'What if I said I'd move over here, live in the staff quarters so your dad would never have to see me if he didn't want to, but he could see Dominic all the time? Hell, I'd even be his servant if that's what he wanted, and he could get his kicks bossing me about.'

Francesco squeezed her hand. 'Don't Kate,' he said, and stood up. 'It would not work.'

'It's worth a shot, isn't it? Can't you ask him?'

He shook his head. 'If I proposed this he would laugh in my face. Besides the fact that 'compromise' isn't a word that has ever featured in his vocabulary, he would believe that I wasn't serious in my intention to oppose him — that it would only be a short space of time before I dropped the case and came round to his own viewpoint.'

Kate hugged herself. 'So that's it? You're telling me that the battle lines are drawn up and to prepare for the massacre?'

'There is one option that I have not told you about. It is the only alternative that I am able to think of.'

'So tell me!'

Despite the urgency of her voice, he seemed in no great hurry to put her out of her misery. He leaned against the trunk of a tree and folded his arms. 'The only solution to this problem that I can think of . . . ' He paused to take a breath. 'The only solution . . . is for you to marry me.'

It was so far removed from anything that Kate had expected him to say, that speech failed her. She searched his face looking for clues, but there were none. It could have been a tailor's dummy staring back at her. She brushed trembling hands through her hair, then dropped her face into her hands.

'You are serious?' She looked up to check several minutes later.

'Perfectly.'

'And you're prepared to chuck your life away on me — when you could have practically anyone you wanted?'

A glimmer of humour broke through the mask, but was quickly extinguished. 'Think one moment before casting me as the hero of the piece, Kate. This arrangement benefits me quite as much as it does you. Do you think I relish the prospect of challenging my father in the courts? Of cannibalising my businesses? Do I really need to provide you with a list?'

'No.' His frankness cut her like a razor, but she had to be grateful that he hadn't attempted to lie about his motives.

'And just by marrying you, all the rest of this would disappear? Whoosh — just like that?' She clicked her fingers.

'Yes.'

'You're certain?'

'I guarantee it.'

'How can you be so sure?'

He unfolded his arms and slipped his hands into his pockets. 'As an unmarried woman, you are very vulnerable in this situation. As a married one, you would have more protection and, as my wife, you would have the greatest. My father would not instigate proceedings against the woman who has married his son. He would be a laughing stock. But even if he does not realise this and decides to continue, I would have the case thrown out of court at the first opportunity.'

Kate twisted her fingers. 'There's no choice then, is there?'

He looked at her coldly. 'There are always choices, Kate, and this one is up to you.' He took his hands out of his pockets. 'And now I have another promise to keep. To your son.'

He began to walk away, then turned back. 'I would appreciate your answer at the earliest opportunity. If I am to marry you, I would much prefer it to be before any scandal breaks.'

Kate watched him go while an immense sadness filtered through to her soul. What she'd received must rank as the cruellest marriage proposal ever.

'Uncle Francesco's building your swing.' She went to collect her son, who raced past her with a whoop of glee. She watched them both from the window and, despite her predicament, she had to admit that she could search for ever without finding anyone who would be as kind to another man's son as Francesco was.

She watched Francesco throw a line of rope over a branch and knot it firmly. At the moment it resembled a hangman's noose. Yeah, right, she had choices. She could either accept his proposal or she go outside and hang herself from his rope.

'Mummy, look!' Dominic was swinging from the rope while Francesco was attempting to cut an old piece of wood to shape with a saw that he'd found.

She smiled at her son. 'You like Uncle Francesco, don't you, Dominic?'

He nodded energetically.

'I've something to tell you.' She waited until he jumped down from the rope, and held out her hand. 'Uncle Francesco is going to be your daddy.' Then she watched with some satisfaction as the wood slipped out of

Francesco's hand and he nearly sliced his finger off.

That was it. She'd told her son, and that was more final in her eyes than any marriage certificate she might sign later. It meant that whatever doubts came to taunt her in the days ahead, there was absolutely no turning back.

Francesco threw the saw on to the ground and came over. 'You're something else, woman,' he hissed in her ear.

She gave him a saccharine sweet smile for the benefit of her son. 'Think you're up to it?'

'I'll have to be, won't I?' he countered, before bending down to Dominic and telling him that he didn't have much practice but he was going to try as hard as he could to be a good daddy. The scene would have melted harder hearts than hers. She certainly couldn't bear it, and left before she had to witness any more.

He came into the living room ten minutes later. 'I can't believe you just did that.'

Neither could she actually, but she wasn't about to admit that to Francesco. 'It must have gone all right.' She pointed out of the window where Dominic was happily swinging on the rope.

'That's not the point! I might have made a total hash of it the way you pushed me into the deep end like that.'

'Sink or swim.' She shrugged. 'You're the best swimmer I know, Francesco.'

'He wants to know if he may call me papa?' he asked brusquely.

A tremor juddered through Kate. She hadn't thought this through. She hadn't thought about anything apart from averting disaster. 'Afterwards. Not until afterwards,' she said.

He acknowledged her words and manner with a curt nod. 'And now you will have to excuse me, I have a marriage to arrange.'

With Dominic's help, she spent the afternoon baking bread. She hadn't done so for years, but as they had nothing left and the phone line was in continual use, it didn't appear that her husband-to-be was going out to get any.

They would talk after dinner, she supposed, and used the last of their fresh meat to cook it.

'Bread nice?' she asked, as he absent-mindedly pulled another piece from the loaf to mop up his gravy.

'Excellent. As was dinner. Thank you.' He stood up and bent over to kiss his nephew on the forehead. 'I'll say goodnight now, Dominic. I'm sorry that I can't play with you at the moment. I'm rather busy.' And with that, he walked out of the kitchen and back to the telephone in the living room.

Kate cleared up, washed the dishes, played with Dominic, then put him to bed. It was nothing she didn't do every night at home, but it felt different. They weren't even married, yet she felt like an abandoned wife whose husband had gone out on the town with his mistress.

It was stupid. She was being petty. She filled the kettle with water and decided to make him a coffee.

'*Grazie*,' he murmured, but it was the way he held out his hand for the drink, while keeping all his attention on the conversation he was conducting, which angered her. It could have been Jack the Ripper slinking into the room and he wouldn't have noticed.

She swore at him.

It seemed to get his attention.

'You can't do this, Francesco.'

He turned back to the receiver. 'I'll phone you back, Vittorio,' he said into it. He stretched his long legs out in front of him and looked up at her. 'I can't do what?'

'You can't blank me out like this. I need to know things.'

He took a sip of his coffee. 'Then ask.'

'OK, when are we getting married?'

'It is not definite yet, but it seems likely that it will be Thursday.'

'This Thursday?' He couldn't be serious.

He nodded.

'I don't know if my parents will be

able to manage that. They're a bit set in their ways.' Kate bit her lip. With her dad's health the way it was, he needed a week's notice before he'd take the car out of the garage to take her mum to Tesco's.

'They will not be attending our wedding, Kate.'

'What?' They'd flip. Her mum would never speak to her again.

'Our wedding must be secret. I assumed you realised that.'

She sat down on the sofa. 'No. No, I didn't.'

'There will be the two of us plus two witnesses. That is all we need. Perhaps I am being ultra-cautious, but I don't want to run the risk of my father discovering what is happening and finding some way to stop us.'

'Dominic?'

He nodded. 'If you wish.'

A thought struck her. 'Won't I need my birth certificate?'

'Vittorio has applied for it.'

'Your dad has my passport. Won't

that be a problem?'

He crossed one leg over the other and she had the distinct impression that he was becoming bored with this conversation. If he yawned, she'd pour the rest of his coffee over him. 'Every problem has a solution, Kate,' he drawled. 'Some take more effort and some take more money, but they can be sorted.'

'And the legal requirement that the banns have to be read so many times? No problem in your case, I take it?'

He raised his eyebrows, but didn't deign to answer.

'It's not right though, is it? One law for the rich and one for the poor?'

He sighed. 'We are doing nothing wrong, Kate. We are both free to marry. If circumstances were different, I would quite happily arrange matters in the conventional manner.'

He checked his watch. 'If that's all, I would like to phone my lawyer back. I expect he will be anxious to return home to his wife.' As he dialled the number, she realised that he'd already forgotten her presence in the room. She knew that it was because he was giving his total concentration to the matter before him. It was an enviable trait, but it didn't make it any easier to handle. The man she'd come to know over the past few days seemed a distant memory. The man she was going to marry was a complete stranger.

19

They were in Florence. Probably one of the most romantic cities in the world in which to marry, but this formed no part of Francesco's decision to go there. Apparently his lawyer's firm had offices in the city and there was a company flat they could use that night. The wedding was set for eleven o'clock the following morning.

'*Ciao*, Vittorio,' Francesco greeted his friend warmly. It was reassuring to see that he could still smile. He'd been so preoccupied the last two days that she'd wondered if he'd lost the ability.

'Kate, Vittorio, my lawyer.' The man stepped forward to greet her, and only because she was waiting for it did she see the very slight hesitation on his part. She looked a mess. There was nothing she could do about it — she hadn't been able to get the soil stains out of her white dress, so the only alternative had been this lemon sundress she'd been wearing the morning they'd escaped from the villa. With no washing machine and no iron, the dress looked as though it had been donated to a third-world country, who'd promptly donated it straight back.

'And this is Dominic.' Kate noted the extra note in Francesco's voice. He'd introduced his nephew with considerably more enthusiasm than he'd introduced her.

Kate watched as Dominic stepped forward solemnly to shake hands. Such gravity in a six-year-old should have been comical. Instead, straight-backed and with his head held proud, Dominic reminded her of an Arab prince receiving homage from one of his subjects.

Vittorio couldn't conceal his surprise. He turned to Francesco and the two men exchanged meaningful looks.

'Paula?' enquired Francesco.

'She is upstairs, making sure that everything is ready in the flat.'

Francesco turned to her. 'So, what would you like to do first?'

'I'm not sure whether to splash out on a new dress for the wedding, or whether this one will do?' she drawled.

Francesco looked startled, and then his eyes widened as he seemed to take in her appearance for the first time. 'You are such a spendthrift, *cara*,' he drawled in exactly the same tone she'd used, his expression daring her to pick him up on the forbidden word. 'You really must try to curb your spending habits when we are married, but as it is a special occasion . . . ' He gave an eloquent Latin gesture.

'I thought you had clothes fittings at two o'clock?' Vittorio looked puzzled.

'Ah yes, completely slipped my mind.' Francesco's lips twitched as he tried not to laugh. He handed her a piece of paper. It was a schedule, with each half hour of the day marked with some activity. Kate knew they had a lot to accomplish in a few hours, and it was probably the only way to ensure that they did it, but she still stared at the list with dismay. Is this what married life would be like with Francesco? She'd have to book an appointment before he'd see her?

'Is that all right?' he asked, already absorbed in some folder that Vittorio had handed him.

'No, it's not.'

Vittorio's head shot up and he studied her with interest. Francesco's was more leisurely; he seemed reluctant to tear himself away from his reading. 'What is it, cara?' he murmured.

'This is no good, caro.' If Francesco was intent on calling her darling, then she'd darling him back until he was heartily sick of it.

He started to laugh. It wasn't exactly the reaction she'd wanted, but at least he'd noticed the jibe. Vittorio gazed from his client to her with utter perplexity.

Francesco sobered quickly. 'In what

way is it no good? I spent a great deal of time arranging it.'

Tell me about it! She told herself grimly. 'I need to go shopping first. Frankly, I'd like to get out of this dress.'

'Fine.' She couldn't believe the speed at which he acquiesced. Her appearance must really have embarrassed him. He traced his finger down the list. 'We'll go for the rings at four o'clock. Arrange it for me, Vittorio, would you?'

Vittorio cast her a look as he got up to obey. She had the distinct impression that he was thinking how she wouldn't get away with being so uppity, if she were marrying him.

'Would you like to leave Dominic here while you go out?'

'If you don't mind. It'd certainly be quicker.'

'I'll call Paula down.'

Kate chewed her lip. She thought he'd been offering to look after her son. Not some woman she'd never met.

He seemed to read her thoughts. 'I'll be here most of the time. He'll be fine.'

And before Paula came in, he handed her an envelope, which she presumed contained money. 'Please don't try to use your credit card.'

She took the money. She had no choice.

Paula was everything she was not. Vittorio's wife looked as though she'd spent the morning in the beauty salon, and the time since perfecting perfection. If this was the model of the ideal Italian wife that Francesco had in mind, then he was in for a bitter disappointment.

'Kate, Paula.' After kissing her affectionately on both cheeks, Francesco performed the introductions, and the two women stared at each other in mutual incomprehension. The poor woman was probably trying to figure out if this was a joke and whether she was supposed to laugh.

'Would you like to come and inspect upstairs?' she asked.

Inspect? What a strange choice of word, and would it be rude to say no because she hadn't much time?

'Kate needs to do some shopping.' Francesco checked his watch. 'You'll need to be back by quarter-to-one, *cara*.'

'I'd better go. Goodbye, *caro*!' She blew Francesco a kiss and gave her son a proper one.

They were sitting around the table in the upstairs flat when she returned at twenty-to-one. Sipping a glass of wine and with his feet propped on a chair, Francesco looked more relaxed than she'd seen him in days. Vittorio and Paula looked like stuffed dummies in comparison.

'Change into these, Dominic.' She threw some carrier bags at her son.

'We saved you some food.' Francesco swept his hand elegantly across the table.

'Brilliant!' She picked up a slice of pizza and bit off a piece. 'Mmm, this is gorgeous.' She tipped up her head and dropped the rest into her mouth.

What? Vittorio and Paula were

staring at her strangely and Francesco's eyes were twinkling as though he were trying not to laugh. 'Does anybody mind if I have the last slice?' she asked, and picked it up before noticing the fine china plates and silver cutlery that the table was set with. Evidently they didn't eat pizza here like she did at home with her friends. She hesitated for a second, wondering whether to put it down and eat it properly, but apart from anything else she didn't have the time. She grinned at Paula. 'Saves on washing up.' And ate the second piece of pizza in exactly the same way.

She was pleased that Francesco had booked an appointment at the hairdressers for her. The sun had dried her hair to the consistency of cornflakes and it was desperately in need of a cut, but as the appointment was for an hour and a half she decided to have some highlights and a conditioning pack as well.

She walked out of the salon to find Vittorio waiting for her. He drove her back to the office, where he ushered her into a downstairs room. She saw the pile of papers on his desk and sat down opposite it. 'Pre-nuptial agreement?' She wondered when they'd be getting around to it. It hadn't been pencilled on Francesco's list of things to do.

'No.' He handed her a folder. 'This is a record of the accounts that my client has opened for you and your son. Also, the amounts that will be paid into them each month.'

Kate glanced at the amounts, and sighed. They were ridiculously large.

'My client would like you to sign this to say that you are in agreement.'

'Call him Francesco please, Vittorio. I am supposed to be marrying him tomorrow,' she snapped, then immediately regretted it. The man was only doing his client's bidding, and she had to admire the way that Francesco had side-stepped all the arguments if he'd been the one to ask her to accept this.

'If you could sign here and here.'

Vittorio handed her his gold fountain pen.

'I don't suppose I have any choice,' she said, taking it.

Vittorio looked affronted. 'Francesco authorised me to tell you that if you wished to argue the amounts you may have more.'

Kate let out a cackle. 'Yeah, that sounds like Francesco. Come on, let's get this over with.' She scrawled her name on the paper.

'And now I am to ask you if you want anything clarifying?'

She nodded. 'The pre-nuptial agreement.'

'There isn't one.'

'You're joking!' As soon as she said it, she realised that Vittorio would never joke about anything so serious. 'Isn't that unusual?'

'Highly unusual.' The poor man looked deeply upset.

Kate sat back and folded her arms. That had truly surprised her.

But she didn't have the chance to ask

Francesco about it. When everything was concluded and they went upstairs, Paula was cooking dinner. Kate, who'd hoped for a quiet evening to try and prepare herself for tomorrow, went to help her.

Quiet and subservient before the men, Paula turned out to be the nosiest person she'd ever met. 'Dominic is the image of Francesco, isn't he?' was her first question.

'He does look a bit like him,' she agreed.

'How long have you known Francesco?' was her next.

Kate, cutting bread, had to turn her head to hide her grin. Subtle, you are not, she thought. 'I first met Francesco seven years ago,' she said, and she could make of that what she would. And would her next question be how old was Dominic?

No. She probably knew that one already. 'Didn't you want a big wedding?' She handed her a glass of Barolo.

Kate took a sip. Was this supposed to loosen her tongue? 'No,' she said. She expected any lawyer of Francesco's to be discreet, but did Vittorio not tell his wife anything? This was becoming embarrassing.

'Will you live in the Villa Mazzoni? It's beautiful up there, isn't it? I'll let you into a secret, Kate. I had hopes at one time of living there . . . '

It was as well that Paula was prattling on and hadn't noticed her reaction. Where on earth were they going to live? It was only one of many questions that they hadn't discussed. Since agreeing on marriage, Francesco had appeared too busy to talk, or was it that he chose not to? Was she destined to be another Paula, not knowing anything about what her husband did?

Paula had gone quiet and was staring at her, waiting for an answer. 'In the short term,' she said.

'Will you miss England?'

Kate grabbed a handful of cutlery. 'I'll set the table, shall I?' Thank goodness dinner was nearly ready.

Paula reverted to form during dinner, and she was treated instead to Vittorio's views on Italian politics and the tax system. Mmm, really riveting stuff! But after Paula's interrogation, strangely soothing. The night wore on but the couple showed no inclination to leave. It was only when Paula unsuccessfully stifled a few yawns and Vittorio shot her a look of disapproval that Kate began to wonder if they were under orders. Had Francesco directed them to stay until the bitter end to prevent any personal discussion between them?

Paranoia? 'I'm sorry, but you'll have to excuse me. I'm shattered. I'll have to go to bed,' she said, and such a look of relief flooded Paula's face that she didn't think it was.

But it was true. She was absolutely exhausted. If she didn't go to bed now, she'd look like Miss Havisham at tomorrow's wedding.

20

Her nerves kicked in the next morning. While her cup clattered in her saucer as she attempted to drink her coffee, she could only be grateful that they'd waited until now to make their presence felt. Everything was done. All she had to do was get herself ready.

Francesco cast her a dark look as he reached for another bread roll. She knew she was getting on his nerves, but she couldn't help it. His life wasn't going to change that much, but she didn't have a clue what she was embarking on. It was his fault. He should have discussed it.

Dominic asked for a glass of orange juice, but she was trembling so much that it slipped out of her hands and splashed over the table.

'For goodness sake, Kate!' Francesco mopped up the mess. 'You're going to the church this morning, not the electric chair.'

She started to cry.

For a moment he hesitated, uncertain, then he held out his hand to Dominic. 'Let's go for a walk and let mama get ready.'

It was easier once he'd gone. She managed to block out all thought apart from the necessity of getting dressed. Her dress cheered her up. She had intended to buy a coat dress or something similar, but once she saw this she knew it was hanging there just waiting for her. It was white silk and had a fitted bodice with tiny blue flowers embroidered on it. The skirt was narrow and dropped in folds to the ground. Lord knows what Francesco would think of it; she looked as though she'd just stepped out of a Pre-Raphaelite painting, but she loved it.

Her flowers were delivered while she was getting ready, and she pulled some out of the bouquet and twisted them among the artificial ones of the simple circular head-dress she'd chosen. It added to the virginal maiden look.

When Francesco returned, she picked up her bouquet and turned to meet him. It stopped him in his tracks.

'You look pretty, Mummy,' said Dominic, but Francesco didn't say a word.

'Well I like it.' She tossed her bouquet on to the table.

He grinned. 'There haven't been many occasions when I have been lost for words, but you took both my breath and my words away.'

'Oh, stick your flattery, Francesco. If you don't like it, just say so.' She turned away from him.

'How could you possibly imagine that I wouldn't like it?'

She glanced up at him. 'Because I look about sixteen in it.'

He shook his head. 'No, but it does emphasise your sweetness and vulnerability. Qualities you don't allow the world to see very often.'

She gazed up at him. He could be so

nice sometimes. Against all the odds, could their marriage have some chance of success?

He held out his hand to Dominic. 'Come, young man, let us also make ourselves beautiful.'

Dominic's outfit was a secret. He'd gone off to the tailor's with Francesco and come back in a fit of giggles. Francesco had shown her the suit he was going to wear — light grey silk, superbly cut, and amazingly soft to the touch — but Dominic had told her that she'd have to wait until tomorrow.

'Are you ready? Close your eyes!' he shouted, and she turned away so she wouldn't be tempted to peek as he came through the door.

'You may look now.' It was Francesco's deep male voice.

She turned. He looked more handsome than she'd ever seen him and, it had to be said, devastatingly sexy. 'Nice,' she murmured, and he made a small bow.

'Where is my page?' he called, and

Dominic entered, a miniature replica of his uncle in similar suit and tie.

'Oh, Dominic!' She dropped to her knees and hugged him. 'You look so grown-up! And now I'm going to cry again.'

'You're not supposed to cry, you're supposed to be happy.'

'It's the same thing,' she said, hugging him tighter.

Francesco gazed down at them fondly. 'You really do look lovely, Kate. We'll make sure that the photographer takes lots of photographs. I would like to commission a portrait of you.'

Kate let out a cry.

'Forgive me, I didn't think.' He slapped himself on the forehead with the heel of his hand. 'What an idiotic thing to say.'

'Oh God.' Until that moment, Kate hadn't given the sentimental portrait that Elizabeth had painted for her and Nico's wedding a thought. She stared down at her dress. No, she couldn't have! What subconscious urge had possessed her to choose something so similar? Even to the flowers twined in her hair. There was no doubting Elizabeth's talent. She'd reached into Kate's soul and guessed exactly the type of dress she'd choose to be married in.

It was too quiet. Kate lifted her head and saw from Francesco's colour-leached face that his thoughts had been rushing along the same path as hers. The only difference being that he thought she'd done this on purpose.

'Francesco, I didn't . . . ' she began, but he thrust up a hand to stop her.

'Don't say one word!' he hissed.

She threw her bouquet to one side. 'I'll go and change.'

He gripped her shoulder to prevent her leaving. 'Why should you? You have made me a happy man, Kate. You have performed a miracle. My dead brother will be attending my wedding.'

'I don't want him there!'

'Oh yes you do.'

He picked up her bouquet and

steered her towards the door. 'Come, let's go.'

'It's too early.'

He gripped her arm more tightly. 'It is because I am so anxious to enter into the state of matrimonial bliss.'

At most weddings it's the bride's mother who cries. At this one it was the bride.

Francesco stood like stone beside her, repeating his vows like an automaton, while she choked hers out between sobs. Beside them, faces steadfastly gazing at the altar, stood Vittorio and Paula. Even through her own misery, she could sense their acute embarrassment. Nobody should be called on to witness such a scene as this, and if ever they met under happier circumstances, she'd do her utmost to make it up to them. All she could be grateful for was that there were no other guests present.

'I always cry when I'm happy.' She clutched her son's hand and hoped that God would forgive her the lie.

They signed the marriage register

and the priest wished them happiness. 'Thank you, father. My wife is a woman like no other,' Francesco answered cryptically.

They drove to the hotel where the five of them were to have lunch and where she and Francesco were staying that night. Before Vittorio and Paula got into their own car to follow, she asked if she could borrow Paula's make-up bag, and spent the short journey trying to repair the damage to her face while Francesco propped his elbow on the window ledge and stared fixedly outside.

The car pulled up outside the hotel and Francesco made to open his door, but Kate grabbed his sleeve. 'I am truly sorry, Francesco,' she said, when he glanced at her.

He picked up a rose that had fallen from her head-dress and threaded it through again. 'Yes, Kate, so am I.'

But he opened her door for her, and offered her his arm to walk into the hotel. She turned to give back Paula's make-up bag and also gave her a smile. She would pull herself together and salvage what was left of this day. For all their sakes.

★ ★ ★

Francesco stretched out his legs, rested his head against the back of the chair and flicked through the TV channels. Vittorio and Paula had gone home, Dominic was next door with a nanny, and they were alone. To outward appearances, Francesco looked relaxed but she knew that he was as tense as she was. This was proved when the phone rang and the remote control scudded out of his hand.

He picked up the receiver, then shifted it slightly away from his ear as an irate voice thundered into the room. 'My father ringing to give us his blessing.' He gave a sardonic smile.

Kate grabbed the room key and headed for the door. 'I'm going to see how Dominic's getting on.' Even from a distance of two hundred miles, Cesare gave her the shivers.

When she returned, Francesco had given up all pretence of watching television and was staring at the blank screen. He looked as grave as she'd ever seen him.

'I don't believe this!' She slammed her key on to the table. 'You promised, Francesco! You said that if I married you, Cesare would back down.'

'Indeed I did.' He continued staring at the screen. 'That was the whole point of our marriage, yes?'

'Yes . . . ' She was missing something here. 'So . . . ?'

'So, it has happened as I said it would.'

'Thank God for that!' Relief rushed through her. 'So where do we go from here?'

He looked up. 'What do you mean?'

'Like where are we going to live when they kick us out of here tomorrow?'

'At the villa.'

She sat on the edge of the sofa and

wrapped her arms around herself. 'Now how did I know you were going to say that?'

'It is one of the conditions.'

'Huh?'

'In exchange for living at the villa with my family, my father has agreed to seek professional help.'

'Great.' Her voice was flat.

'As my wife, you will be treated with respect and courtesy by everyone there, including my father.'

'And he's agreed to that as well, has he?'

'He has.'

She wasn't convinced. 'Can I take a video?'

'You should be pleased. If he doesn't uphold his part of the bargain, we move out, and you may choose where we live.'

She considered his grave expression. 'And shouldn't you be a bit more pleased about it? Haven't you got everything you wanted?'

He gave her a strange look, then rapped his knuckles against the side of the chair. 'It gives me no pleasure to see my father reduced to this.'

'No, I suppose not, but it's been a long time coming, hasn't it?'

'Indeed. And I blame myself for not ensuring that my father received the help he needed sooner.'

He looked so sad at that moment that, before she could think, she sat down on the floor beside him and wrapped her arms around his knees. 'It's not your fault, Francesco. Have you ever met anyone until now that could get your dad to do anything he didn't want to? From what I've seen of him, it would take the SAS to kidnap him before he'd even begin negotiations.'

There was a quirk of a smile. 'You are kind to say so . . . ' He hesitated for a moment. ' . . . Signora Mazzoni.'

Mmm, this was something they should address. She patted his knee. 'I think I'll go for a bath.'

Twenty minutes later, what had seemed the sensible thing to do now struck her as absolutely terrifying. Twenty minutes after that, as she stared at the wisp of material that pretended to be a night-dress, she was still shaking. And twenty minutes further on, she wondered why he wasn't demanding if she'd been sucked down the plughole.

'Are you all right, Kate?' It took another twenty minutes before Francesco's honeyed tones penetrated the barrier between them.

Kate gulped all the remaining air of the bathroom into her lungs, reminded herself that she'd obtained an 'A' in GCSE Drama, and flung the door open. '*Si, Signor Mazzoni.*' As she did so, the situation struck her as such as cliché that a gurgle of laughter rose to her throat. She couldn't blame Francesco if he laughed at her. She'd join in, and they could relax.

Francesco wasn't laughing. She wasn't certain what was going on in his head until the male hormones defeated everything else, and his eyes began to scan her body as though looking for hidden weapons.

'You know exactly what this is doing to me, don't you?'

Kate wasn't certain why he sounded angry. Perhaps it was because she'd insulted his intelligence. A bloke would have to be brain dead not to get the point of this attire.

But as she was wondering whether to give up and shut herself back in the bathroom, he pulled her to him and his mouth closed on hers. His lips forced hers open and his tongue seized the advantage. Questing fingertips roved down her back, pressing her irresistibly closer to him, then one hand held her in the desired position while another moulded itself around her breast.

Kate reeled at the suddenness of it, but decided against protesting. A woman wearing what she was, had little right to demand subtlety from her lover.

Even that barrier was being swiftly removed. He hooked a finger under the straps, lifted them over her shoulder and allowed gravity to complete the task for him. For several moments his eyes feasted on what he'd uncovered, then he drew her to him, fusing the length of their bodies together.

She felt his arousal like a rock trying to embed itself into her stomach, ready and waiting as soon as its owner gave the word. Her heart started to thud. Who was this man who was taking such liberties with her body? He was her husband. Yet she probably knew more about the man who ran her corner shop than she did about him.

'Come.' He took her hand and pulled her towards the bedroom. She took a deep breath and tried to still her fears. She was about to learn a whole lot more about Francesco than she ever would about Mr Patel.

The satin cover felt cold against her back as Francesco picked her up and placed her on the bed. She started to tremble as he kicked off his shoes and knocked the phone from its cradle so that they wouldn't be disturbed. Lord, did he mean to take her now? She wasn't ready.

She wasn't certain what his intentions were. All she knew was that she was lying there like a dish of the day that his eyes had already devoured most of. He stood at the end of the bed, unbuttoning his shirt as he watched her, then he knelt and began to kiss the tender flesh of her inner thighs, slowly but purposefully moving upwards.

Relax. She repeated the words to herself, hoping that her brain would eventually take some notice and act on it. She was certain that she would have, given more time, but her body was still tense when he lifted his head.

'Would you like me to stop, Kate?' He gazed deep into her eyes, searching for something only he suspected was there.

'No.' Let them get this over with. It wasn't exactly what she'd hoped her wedding night would be, but then neither had her wedding day.

'Are you sure?' As he spoke, he allowed his fingers to wander sensually across her thighs, and she arched her back with the sensation. They could be good together. She was certain of it. Maybe not this time. Maybe they were both too uptight for that. But in the future. In her mind, if they could only get over the obstacle of their first time, they would be all right.

'Please.' Let him do it. She didn't want to go through this again. She closed her eyes to concentrate better on the pleasurable sensation of his fingers against her flesh.

'Please?'

'Just do it, Francesco! Please!' What did he want? For her to beg?

'Just do it?' As his hands pinned her shoulders to the bed and the force of his words scorched her face, she realised, belatedly, that it wasn't the most romantic thing to say to any male. Especially not an Italian one.

Her eyes snapped open and she gazed at him in fright.

'Just do it!' he repeated, and she had to admit that the more he said it the worse it sounded. 'While you do what, *cara*?' His face came closer and his eyes glinted with rage. 'While you close your eyes and think of another man inside you?'

21

Kate put on her dressing gown and wandered around their hotel suite. She had no idea where Francesco was. He'd pulled his clothes on last night and stormed out of the room. The last time she'd looked, at five o'clock this morning, he still hadn't returned. It was now seven, and the situation hadn't changed.

'Where on earth have you been?' she said, when he walked into the room at half-past-seven.

He gave a wry smile. 'Walking. Thinking. It is a beautiful city.'

'You could have been mugged.'

'I wasn't.'

'I thought I was going to have to pawn my wedding ring to get out of here.'

He walked over to her, and tipped her chin gently upwards so that she would look at him. 'I apologise for worrying you and for my outburst last night, Kate. Will you forgive me?'

She nodded, truly grateful that he'd come back and that he didn't seem angry any more. And, as it seemed to be apology time . . . she murmured, 'Will you forgive me?'

'There is nothing to forgive.' He kissed her briefly on the tip of her nose and let her go. 'You cannot help still being in love with my brother.'

She groaned. 'I'm not, Francesco! How can I make you believe that?'

'When I see it in your eyes. When I look into them and see the same emotion there as I see when you look at your child or speak of my brother.'

'Last night . . . '

'Was a fiasco. You have the body of a goddess, cara, but I knew that you weren't offering that body to me freely. I felt as though I had bought you. Without our bargain, my bed would have been the last place you'd have lain in.'

'Sorry.' She had no idea that he was so sensitive. Caught up in breaking down the barrier between them last night, she hadn't attempted to look at things from his perspective at all. The last thing he'd needed was her bursting out of the bathroom dressed like a whore. Well done Kate.

Tentatively, she reached out and touched his arm. It felt as though there was a force-field between them. Tonight, she supposed, they'd have to try and break through it all over again. 'Maybe next time?'

He took her hand and pressed it to his lips. 'Next time will be perfect, I promise you.'

Oh? There was nothing like confidence in a man. She hoped he was right and she certainly wasn't going to contradict him, but he seemed to have come to terms very easily with the fact that she was still supposed to be in love with Nico.

* * *

Francesco apologised for the fact that they couldn't stay longer in Florence, and also that he wouldn't be driving them back to Rome himself. When he told her that he'd hired a driver, she supposed it was because he wanted to sleep in the car. Instead, he spent the whole journey discussing business on his mobile phone. She waited for him to declare that this marriage business had seriously messed up his schedule. But he didn't have to. It was patently obvious.

Was this to be her life? A husband who gave himself to her in little chunks, in between his business commitments? She trailed a finger along the base of the window and stared at the dirt it had picked up. Beside her, Francesco appeared to be booking up every single hour of every single day for the rest of this month with business meetings. What time did that leave for them? And if he was so sensitive, how come he hadn't figured that you couldn't neglect a woman all day and still expect shooting stars at night?

Kate sighed, took a tissue out of her bag and wiped her finger. After everything that had happened, it was ridiculous to yearn for an ideal of marriage that probably didn't exist. Maybe this was as good as it got — a rich husband who was doing his best to be nice to her.

She reached over and cuddled Dominic. He was putting words into a personal organiser that Francesco had given him and she could see that he wasn't too pleased at being interrupted, but he submitted to her attentions with good grace. At least in Italy, mothers could show open affection to their children. The poor boy would have to put up with this for as long as she had the energy to catch him.

Francesco caught the action and smiled warmly at her. 'Happy?' he whispered.

'Mmm.' Considering the alternative, it wasn't too much of a lie.

Kate's heart began to pound as they

crunched along the gravel drive and she caught sight of the Villa Mazzoni once more. It would be some time before she could look at it and not recall the terror that had possessed her when she left it last.

'You don't have to do this now,' Francesco said, as they tramped towards his father's study.

'Oh no, I wouldn't miss this.' She wasn't going to scurry around the corridors of her new home in fear of meeting its owner. Done that. Been there. Now she wanted the T-shirt with 'I survived Cesare Mazzoni' written on the front.

He was waiting for them, seated on a leather chair by the window. Immediately his eyes sought hers, blazing their continued hate across the few yards that separated them. Instinctively, she grabbed Francesco's hand and felt it close around her own, protecting her and reassuring her that she was safe. Lord, she was pleased he'd been on her side. Cesare was a formidable foe and, without the intervention of his son, he'd have crunched her up and spat her out by now.

'Father.' Francesco's tone was mild, but there was no doubting the warning it contained. There was also no doubting the effort it took for Cesare to blank out his true feelings and plaster a smile on his face.

'May I present my bride, Kate.'

To her astonishment, Cesare managed to kiss her on both cheeks, though she wasn't keen on having his bony jaws quite so close to her jugular vein.

'You are welcome. My home is your home. I hope you will be very happy here.'

'Thank you, Papa.' Francesco answered for her as she was incapable of speech. 'We owe you a great debt. If circumstances had not thrown us together as they did, we would never have discovered our love for each other.'

The expression on Cesare's face was priceless. Now she knew the effort it had cost him to appear pleasant, because she was experiencing the same trying not to laugh. Perhaps Francesco's remark was a little below the belt, but she could have hugged him for it.

Her moment of triumph was brief. Francesco suggested that they leave Dominic with his grandfather while he showed her their rooms. She followed him to a different wing of the villa to the one she'd occupied and gazed around intently as he opened the door of his room. Mmm, it was nice enough, but too darkly masculine. She wondered if he'd mind her at least painting the walls a lighter colour.

'There is a living room, bathroom, study, guest room.' He pointed down the corridor. 'Feel free to rearrange them as you will. Perhaps you'd like a kitchen installed?' He shrugged.

'Yeah, maybe.'

'And next door . . . ' He opened the door of another bedroom.

'Is Dominic's room,' she said brightly.

He waited until she'd gone into the

room and was looking around wondering why there weren't any toys in it before he came in and closed the door. 'Is your room, Kate,' he said quietly.

'Mine?' It was a lovely room, but that wasn't the point.

'Again, please feel free to change anything you wish.'

'We're married, Francesco,' she reminded him.

'Yes.'

'So what are your servants going to think? I thought you worried about stuff like that.'

He walked over to the window, leaned his arm against it and gazed out. 'They will think nothing of it. My mother and father had separate rooms, yet they still managed to produce three children.'

'Three?' She sat down smartly in an armchair.

He turned to look at her. 'Nico didn't tell you?'

'No.'

'You surprise me.'

She shook her head. 'It doesn't surprise me, Francesco. Look who he had as a role model.'

He chose to ignore her. 'Unfortunately Giacamo died when he was barely three months old. No recognisable cause.'

'Oh.'

'Nico was born a year later. There were complications at his birth and mama was told that she couldn't have any more children. Perhaps because of this and because of the child they'd lost, my parents . . . '

'Spoiled him rotten.' She finished the sentence for him when he hesitated.

'He was indulged, yes. Especially by my mother.'

'I know this now, Francesco. I couldn't see it then because I was infatuated with him. It wasn't love. It was obsession. Do you believe me?'

His eyebrows lifted in surprise as she spoke, but he only shrugged in answer.

Kate sighed. Maybe if she kept telling him, one day he'd believe her. But, back to the matter in hand. 'Why separate rooms, Francesco?' she appealed.

He came over, pulled her to her feet, and gripped her hands in his. 'Do you really think I could lie in the same bed as you, *cara*, and not make love to you?'

She stared at him. 'But isn't that rather the point?'

'You didn't want me, Kate.'

She groaned. 'Look, I've said I was sorry about the way I acted last night. It was the first time. I was nervous . . . '

He placed his finger over her lips. 'I am not seeking another apology. There is no blame attached to any of this. All I ask is the answer to one question — if I'd asked you to marry me before all of this happened, what would your answer have been?'

'Oh, Francesco . . . ' She looked away.

'I have my answer.'

'But we are married. It's different!'

'No difference.' He touched her fingers to his mouth and brushed them gently against his lips. 'It is difficult for me to explain this.'

'Try.' Was it simply because he'd told her that he wouldn't make love to her that her body was stirring now? What quirk of nature wanted her to coil her arms around his neck, press her body against his, and make him change his mind? She pulled away from him. It might work. And she might be driven to try it sometime. But not now.

'For years, people have asked me why I haven't married. I knew the answer but I have never told anyone.'

'Go on.' He certainly had her attention.

'I was seeking the perfect woman.'

She started to laugh.

'You laughed once before when I told you I was a romantic.'

She remembered.

'We always laugh at that which we secretly are.'

'That's a bit deep.'

'But true.'

'I'm about as far from romantic as you can possibly get,' she said.

He raised his eyebrows but didn't comment further.

'So what's your perfect woman like?'

He smiled. 'Someone beautiful, intelligent, witty and caring. Someone who would love me for myself and not my money. And someone who, after fifty years of marriage, I would never be quite certain what she was thinking or going to say next.'

'Wow! You don't ask for much, do you? No wonder you never found anyone for the job.'

'I thought I'd found her at one time.'

'When was that then?'

He shook his head. 'Kate, you can be so dense at times.'

'You're joking!' She started to laugh but stopped abruptly when he looked hurt. 'OK, I've got the same question for you. If I'd asked you to marry me before all this happened what would your answer have been?'

'I would have said that, because of our past history, we needed to take things slowly and discover more about each other before taking such a big step.'

'Oh.' There had been times when she'd thought he liked her a little bit or was physically attracted to her, but never like this. Perhaps he was right. Perhaps she was dense. 'So what now?' She threw her hands into the air.

'Now we do it as it should have been done. I've waited a long time to find you, *cara*, so a little longer should not be so difficult. I promised you that when I took you to bed next it would be perfect. And it will be, for the next time you find yourself there, it will be because you love me and you will want, heart and soul, to be there.'

'How will you know?'

He smiled. 'That's easy. I will see it in your eyes.'

She wandered around the room, opening drawers and cupboards but not seeing inside. Love. Would she ever love him? She liked him sometimes but at other times she found him infuriating. He made her laugh, but he'd also made her cry. He could be kind, but she'd witnessed his cruelty. He was the sexiest man she'd ever met. She kicked the wardrobe door closed. Love. It wasn't bits and pieces of things. It was a wholeness, a completeness. You knew when you were in love.

'What if it never happens?' she asked.

It seemed to be the question he was waiting for. 'Then we enjoy what we have, Kate,' he said as he left the room.

And it wasn't until he'd gone and she was pondering his words that she realised that, during all his talk of love, he'd never once said he loved her.

22

She supposed she should be grateful. He did at least stop what he was doing and give her his full attention when she interrupted him at work. She'd been to the Villa Giulia Museum and decided to call into his office to see whether he was free for lunch. Hope sprang eternal, even in her breast.

'Sorry, *cara*.' His face twisted into an expression of suitable disappointment. 'I have a meeting in twenty minutes. If you'd rang earlier, I could have rearranged it.'

'Sorry, I should have made an appointment,' she muttered.

He was on his feet in an instant. He stood before her and cupped her face in his hands. 'I am trying.'

'Very trying.'

He smiled. 'It can't be so bad if you can still joke about it.'

She sighed. 'I don't see you, Francesco. I can't believe how you managed to clear your diary for the week of our visit and the week afterwards.'

'I am still paying for it.'

She wrenched away from him and ran out of his office. She knew he wouldn't follow her. That his wife was running along the corridors of the Mazzoni head office was bad enough. That he should be seen chasing her was impossible.

Her mobile phone rang at intervals all afternoon. Each time she looked and saw who it was, she decided not to answer it.

She was towelling her hair dry after playing with Dominic in the pool when he arrived home early that evening. As he strode towards them, severe in his formal business attire, Kate put down the towel and prepared herself for a row. She wasn't looking forward to this. She knew she'd been childish, but she was unhappy.

'Dominic!' Francesco picked him up as he ran towards him, turned him upside down and pretended he was going to throw him in the pool. With her son's yells renting the air, he continued on towards her, laid Dominic on a sun lounger and kissed her briefly.

'I knew you would turn this exact shade.' He trailed a fingertip through the rivulets of moisture running down her arm. 'My golden goddess.'

Kate tipped her face up to scrutinise his. She'd expected anger not flattery.

He was already turning away, pulling at his tie and shrugging out of his jacket. 'I have been looking forward to this all day,' he said, heading for the pool house.

He returned a minute later, but she had little time to admire the tightly-honed contours of his body before he flung himself into the pool. Dominic made to follow him, but Kate called him back. Francesco was powering through the water like a torpedo and would have sunk him if they'd come into contact. These weren't the leisurely lengths he usually enjoyed after a hard day's work — this was a man working through something with sheer physical exertion.

Eventually he stopped, and Kate picked up a towel and walked over to him.

'*Ciao, cara.*' He took the towel and rubbed it briskly over his body.

'You've done it, Francesco. Congratulations.'

He frowned. 'I have done what?'

Kate grimaced. Why did she always do this? Here the man was working himself up to a serious discussion or argument with her, and here she was cracking jokes. No wonder he spent every spare minute working. If their positions were reversed, she'd irritate the hell out of her as well.

'I have done what?' he repeated.

'Qualified for the next Olympics,' she said flatly.

'Ah.' He raised an eyebrow, and continued drying himself.

She no longer thought it was funny either. 'Dominic go and find *nonno*. He wants to hear all the new Italian words you've learned.'

As she knew he would, her son made a fuss and protested vociferously about going.

'Dominic, do as mama tells you,' said Francesco and, pulling a face, Dominic went.

'This isn't working with my father?' he asked, watching the stiff little figure marching off.

'Yeah, it's fine. He'd just rather be with you, that's all.'

'And you and Cesare?'

Kate shrugged. 'We managed to sit at the same table for lunch today, and I didn't catch him looking at me in a strange way. Ten out of ten for effort, I suppose.'

'Yes, lunch . . . ' Francesco picked up her mobile phone from the table and handed it to her. 'You must get this checked out, Kate. I tried ringing you but there was no reply.'

Kate stared at him. They both knew that there was nothing wrong with her phone.

'After you'd gone, I realised that lunch with you was a far more exciting prospect than a dull business meeting. I intended to rearrange it if I'd been able to contact you.'

Kate sat on the sun lounger and folded her arms. He was clever, her husband, telling her something that she couldn't possibly check.

Francesco sat on the bottom of the lounger and lifted her legs over his lap. 'There has never been one moment when I've regretted the time I spent with you at the villa and then at the house by the river,' he said, running his fingers over the downy hairs of her upper thigh.

'But it played havoc with your business.' She tried to block out how pleasurable his touch was.

'Yes! I have already said.' He threw his hands into the air. 'Am I supposed to lie to you?'

She drew her knees up to her chin. 'No.'

He shifted closer. 'For the next two weeks, I am going to be incredibly busy. Why don't you visit your parents?'

'No.' They'd gone the week after the wedding and Kate could still recall their utter bewilderment and concern for her. Even though Francesco was charm itself — and she'd given an 'A'-star performance, about how they'd fallen in love and couldn't help themselves getting married in such a romantic place as Florence — she knew it hadn't convinced her parents. She rang them frequently to tell them that she was happy, and this seemed to keep their worries at bay. Although she missed them terribly, she wouldn't visit them and allow them to see through her act.

'This isn't working.' Francesco got up and raked a hand through his hair.

'No. I need to get a job. If I was working, maybe I wouldn't mind you not being around so much.'

Francesco looked hurt. 'Where will you work?'

'Depends who'd have me.'

'I would employ you.'

Kate smiled. That would be one way of seeing more of your husband — work for him. 'I'll have to wait a while anyway. I want to be around when Dominic starts his new school next month. It's going to be a major change for him.'

'He will be fine.'

She nodded. He probably would. It only seemed to be her that was worrying about it.

'The last thing I ever wanted was to make you unhappy,' he said suddenly.

Struck by the sadness that permeated his expression and posture, Kate got up and kissed his cheek. 'I know, Francesco. I'm sorry. The last thing I ever wanted was to be a whining wife.'

He took her in his arms and pressed her to him. The chilliness of the declining day evaporated as the heat from his body merged with her own. His mouth sought hers and her lips parted in welcome. It was so achingly sweet when he kissed her like this, but she always felt so devastatingly empty when he pulled away, as he did now. She knew it wasn't because he didn't want her. He was a man and couldn't conceal the evidence of his desire. He'd told her why he was doing it but, oh God, it didn't help.

His face was serious as he picked up a wrap and held it out to her. He gazed at the ground, then slowly shook his head as he looked at her again. 'I'm sorry, Kate. It was a mistake.'

Panic like a poisoned arrow speared her heart. No, he couldn't give up on her! Yes, she'd been a real pain and, yes, she'd given him a hard time about their marriage, but they could put that behind them. She'd try harder. Honestly, she would.

The strength of her emotions dazed her and she sat abruptly down on a chair. Then she covered her face with her hands. If he was about to tell her that this marriage was over before it had even begun, then he wasn't going to witness the effect his words had.

23

'It was a mistake,' he repeated, as though once through the heart wasn't enough. 'I should have told you my plans instead of battling ahead with them.'

He crouched down in front of her and lifted her hands away from her face. 'I wanted it to be a surprise, but it hasn't worked.'

'What was meant to be a surprise?' She was totally confused.

'Our honeymoon.'

Of all the things she'd expected him to say, this was furthest from her imagination.

'It had to be before Dominic started school, so I knew I didn't have much time to clear my diary like I did before, but because of my previous absence it has proved more difficult.'

She started to cry, and his arms came

around her. 'Why didn't you tell me?' she sobbed, instantly guilty about all the things she'd thought and said about his work.

'I was looking forward to seeing your face when I told you where we were going. Please don't cry, Kate.' He held her tighter. 'I never meant to upset you.'

'Where are we going?' Her curiosity overcame the warm feeling of security she garnered, snuggled into his neck.

He sat back on his heels and grinned. 'I have chartered a yacht that, in fifteen days time, will take us on a cruise along the Amalfi coast. We shall stop at Pompeii, Sorrento, the island of Capri, and anywhere else you wish.'

She clasped her hands together and her eyes glowed. 'Oh gosh, Francesco, that's so romantic!'

He grinned again. 'Not that you would know or care for such things.'

She stuck out her tongue, then changed her mind and kissed him on the cheek. 'I'm sorry for spoiling it. It would have been a lovely surprise. It is a lovely surprise!'

'In that case it is not spoiled.' He stood up and pulled her with him. 'I have something to ask you.'

'OK.'

'My mother is keen to visit before we go away. Do you have any objections?'

'Of course I don't. Why should I?'

'She feels responsible for what happened. She told me to tell you that she will understand if you don't want to see her.'

'Oh, Francesco.' Kate shook her head in amazement. 'I thought she hadn't been in touch because she was working like crazy. She struck me as the type of person who would forget everything once she got into her studio.' She didn't tell him that she'd been secretly miffed by Elizabeth's silence. She should have known that she'd jumped to the wrong conclusion yet again.

He gave a wry smile. 'I shall tell her that we would all like to see her.'

'Can I tell her?'

He nodded. 'That would be even better.'

'Francesco?'

'Hmm?'

'What did the people at your work think about me running out of your office today?'

'I doubt they thought anything.'

'How come?' She wasn't certain what to make of the smile twitching at the corner of his lips.

'You are English, Kate. They expect such strange behaviour of your race.'

Laughing, he walked away, so wasn't aware of the flipflop flying through the air until it hit him in the centre of his back.

★　★　★

'This is perfect, Francesco.' She hoped that it *was* Francesco, because whoever was standing behind her, had lifted the hair from her neck and was kissing the flesh which he'd revealed.

She turned away from the sea. It

meant missing the last glimpse of Mount Vesuvius as they sailed across the Bay of Naples towards Capri, but the sight of her husband, tanned and relaxed in T-shirt and shorts, was fair compensation. She twined her arms around his neck, offered up her mouth to be kissed, and waited for the surge of longing that would overcome her as he bent to do her bidding.

It came as it always did, surprising her each time by the force of her need for this man. Always the desire seemed stronger than the last time. Could it be possible?

He drew away from her, breathing rapidly, but she clung to him. Her bones had liquefied and she didn't think she could stand without his support. 'Take me below,' she murmured. It was the first time she'd openly asked him to make love to her. She'd determined not to, but she wanted him so much.

'Kate.' He rested his cheek against hers. She could feel his breathing returning to normal while hers only seemed more ragged.

'Do you love me, Kate?' He lifted up his head to gaze at her.

He was willing her to say yes, but would he believe her if she did? And was she in love with him? Yes, she was desperate for him to make love to her, but that wasn't exactly the same thing. So how would she know the moment it happened? Would it be — oh, yes, the thirty-first of August, that was the day I fell in love with Francesco. It was a daft idea. It didn't happen like that.

'Do you love me, Francesco?' she answered instead.

His eyes crinkled as he smiled. 'I asked you first.'

They had reached stalemate. Kate lifted her eyes to the heavens for inspiration, but instead saw a sight that scudded every other thought from her brain. Maria was leaning over the railings of the upper deck, giggling with a member of the crew.

'Where's Dominic, Maria?' she shouted.

'Sorry, *Signora*.' The girl shielded her eyes from the sun and peered down. 'Dominic is with *Signor* Mazzoni.'

She felt a judder run through Francesco. 'Maria?' he demanded.

The girl's face paled. '*Signor*? Dominic said he was going to find you.'

'You can't have let him go off like that, Maria!' Kate was beside herself. This wasn't the villa, where she knew that he could wander around safely. This was a ship, with plenty of ways in which a curious child could get into trouble.

Francesco cut her short. 'When was this, Maria?'

'A-about twenty minutes ago.'

Kate thought she was going to choke. She seemed to have forgotten how to breathe, and the air that she managed to drag into her lungs sounded like the rasp of a death rattle.

'He is all right, Kate.' Francesco gripped her arms.

'He's not . . . he's not! I've got such a bad feeling about this. I never should have let him out of my sight. I never should have brought him on a damned boat!'

'Stop it, Kate.' Francesco gripped harder. 'You couldn't have kept him away from the sea all his life. He is all right. I have a good feeling about it. He's probably lying on his bunk drawing. You check below, while I'll check up here.'

Kate ran off as, behind her, Francesco issued orders to scour the decks for her son. Despite all his apparent confidence, however, he was leaning over the handrail scanning the water when she glanced back.

'Have you seen Dominic recently?' she asked of anyone she passed, but the answer was always *no*.

Please, please, Dominic, be in there, she prayed fervently as she approached his cabin. She'd be the perfect mother for the rest of her life. She'd never . . . ever . . . shout at him again.

The cabin was empty. She snatched the battered teddy from his pillow and hugged it to her. It smelled of him and she placed it back. For years, she'd taken an old shirt of Nico's to bed with her. The smell had faded but the memory hadn't. It couldn't be repeating again. It would destroy her if the same thing happened with his son.

'It will be all right.' She said Francesco's words like a chant to ward off evil. There were plenty of places a child could hide on this vessel. Dominic was in one of them. She had to believe it or her sanity would snap.

She checked every possible place that a small child could conceal himself before climbing the steps to the deck. They'd have found him by now. If they hadn't . . .

'Kate?' Francesco spun round as he heard her coming.

She shook her head and staggered over to him. There was no mistaking the expression on his face. Her ultra-confident husband was worried out of his skull. He held her to his chest and she heard the blood thundering through it. 'No . . . ' she moaned, her tears soaked his T-shirt.

'*Signor?*' One of the crew pointed out to sea.

Francesco snatched up the binoculars, gazed through them for a second and threw them down. She picked them up, but could only see an indistinguishable blob in the water.

Francesco gave the order to turn about and began kicking off his shoes and wrenching off his T-shirt and shorts.

Kate reminded herself of how good a swimmer Dominic was, and tried to block out the fact that he was only six, that he'd only ever swam in a pool, and of how long he must have been in the sea. It didn't work. With a moan, she bent over and began tearing at her own shoes.

'No, Kate.' Francesco pulled her up and guided her to one of the crew. 'Giancarlo, whatever you do, do not allow my wife to go in the water.'

'Sorry, *Signora*,' said the man,

holding her fast. She was glad of his support a moment later when she saw Francesco climb on to the handrail and dive overboard. She buried her face in the sailor's chest and prayed. She didn't want to watch her husband swimming, she didn't want to see what he found; all she wanted was to see him when he brought her son back to her. Alive.

'Mummy . . . ?' A small voice penetrated her prayers. She shivered. Francesco couldn't possibly have achieved that yet. It was her imagination. She didn't believe in ghosts.

'Sorry, Mummy,' said the voice again. Then . . .

'*Signora* Mazzoni?' It was Maria. 'I found him, *Signora*! He was in the tender. We looked before but he was hiding under the awning. He seemed to think we were playing hide-and-seek.'

Kate hazarded a glance downwards. Yes . . . it *was* her son, flesh and blood, and not her imagination. His dark eyes were wide as he gripped Maria's hand and tried to hide behind her skirt.

'Dominic! Don't you ever, ever, *ever* do anything like that again!' she shouted, and with this outburst her rage vanished. Her child was safe. Nothing else mattered.

She dropped to her knees. 'Come here, you.' She outstretched her hands, grabbed him, and hugged the breath out of him.

'I'll never do anything like that again, *Signora*. I'll never leave him by himself,' Maria promised.

Kate looked up. 'Has anybody told Francesco that Dominic is safe?' she asked, but was met by blank faces. She hurried to the handrail and looked overboard. There was no sign of her husband and, from this distance, the blob he'd been swimming towards was clearly an old shirt caught on a piece of driftwood.

'Giancarlo?' The rest of the crew were either sauntering back to their jobs or making a fuss of Dominic.

The man looked out to sea. 'He's not there, *Signora*.'

'I know that!' Kate screamed. 'Where is he?'

One of the men stopped. '*Signor* Mazzoni?' He looked puzzled. 'Hasn't he come back on board?'

Kate shook her head, and then tore around the crew. Once Dominic had been found, it seemed that no one had given a thought to the man who might be struggling for his life in the sea.

'No.' Kate felt her world shatter. Her old enemy had fooled her completely. It had no interest in claiming the life of her son. Its sole purpose was to take the man she loved.

She sank to the deck, hugged her knees, and whimpered softly. This was too much to bear. Even with a child to act as a focus, she didn't think she could survive this.

'*Cara?*' If it hadn't been for the drops of water splashing down on her, Kate doubted whether she'd ever have believed that Francesco was real.

'I thought I'd lost you,' she gasped.

He gave a wry smile. 'I'm not that

easy to lose.' He sat on the deck beside her and held out his arms. She snuggled inside them and allowed herself to be soothed and stroked back to sanity. She didn't ever want to move. Even if Vesuvius erupted and belched its lava over them — she knew that she'd be quite happy to be held within his warm embrace, like this, for the rest of eternity.

And then he began to kiss her. Softly at first, but then, as she responded ardently to him, with an urgency which he'd never shown before.

'I want you, Kate. I never believed I could want anyone so much.'

Thank the Lord for that, Kate told herself ecstatically, closing her eyes and allowing the tremors of desire to flow swiftly through her body. This time they would be assuaged.

She moaned as his lips pressed scorchingly hot kisses down her neck, and she cried out loud as he found the exact spot which increased the sensation a thousandfold.

'What about my eyes?' She hung limply as he gathered her into his arms and carried her below, to his bed. Her bones had melted, replaced by a warm golden honey that flooded her body with sweet longing.

'Your eyes are the most beautiful ones I have ever seen.' He kissed each one. 'They tell me everything I want to know.' He closed the door on the world and stripped off her clothes.

She lay languorously on the bed and smiled up at him as he simply stood looking down at her. He was the most beautiful thing she'd ever seen . . . and the most brave, the most wonderful. 'I love you, Francesco,' she said, unable to stop the words bursting out.

'I love you, Kate,' he said, and her heart filled with even more love. He lay beside her and gathered her close. 'I have a secret to confess.'

'Oh . . . ?' Her voice was slightly high-pitched, as he'd chosen this moment to slide a hand between her legs and uncover another erogenous

401

zone. 'Oh,' she said again, and this time it wasn't a question. She was simply discovering another area in which her new husband excelled.

'Don't you want to know my secret?' he taunted, as the tension grew and she arched against him.

'No. Not really.' There was a time and a place for everything, and she knew exactly what time it was now. She silenced him with a kiss and, thankfully, he read her mind and positioned himself above her.

'There is no rush, *cara*.' He caressed her breasts and seemed in no hurry to put her out of her misery.

'Oh, yes there is!' She'd been starved of her husband for too long. Maybe next time she'd sample the starter and hors d'oeuvres. However, *this* time, she craved the main course. She coiled her arms around his neck and lifted her hips up to touch his, Francesco's resolve shattering the moment she began moving sensually against him.

'Something tells me that I shall never

be able to deny you anything your heart desires,' he murmured, and thrust into her. Her fingers twisted through the tight coils of hair at the nape of his neck and dragged him closer as she exulted in the sensation of his masculinity deep within her. Her muscles gripped the whole glorious length of him. No, he would never deny her this again.

What at first was an achingly slow rhythm became stronger and more insistent as their passion increased. She marvelled that he knew by instinct exactly the right pace she needed. She clung to him as he brought her to the very edge of fulfilment, torn between not wanting this moment between them ever to cease and her natural longing to reach the other side. He controlled her totally, and in this area she acknowledged his mastery and offered submission. The ripples of pleasure pulsing through both their bodies told her that the time was soon. Oh God, she hoped it was soon. She didn't think she could bear it much more. 'I love you, Francesco,' she moaned, and they hurtled into oblivion together.

The light was fading when she stretched herself like a pampered feline against the length of his body. 'You were right,' she purred.

'Hmm?' He raised himself on his elbow to look at her.

'It was perfect.'

His dark eyes glistened. 'Yes it was. I love you, Kate.'

The words flowed over her like a precious healing balm. She smiled up at him. 'Did you mention something about a secret or was it my imagination?'

He gave a deep chuckle. 'I just wanted you to know that I loved you first.'

She traced her finger around his wide sensual lips. 'Shall I tell you a secret?'

'That would be nice.' He kissed the tip of her finger and sucked it gently into his mouth.

'On the thirty-first of August, I fell in

love with my husband.'

He grinned. 'No secret,' he said, and pulled her into his arms.

THE END

We do hope that you have enjoyed reading this large print book.

Did you know that all of our titles are available for purchase?

We publish a wide range of high quality large print books including:
**Romances, Mysteries, Classics
General Fiction
Non Fiction and Westerns**

Special interest titles available in large print are:
**The Little Oxford Dictionary
Music Book, Song Book
Hymn Book, Service Book**

Also available from us courtesy of Oxford University Press:
**Young Readers' Dictionary
(large print edition)
Young Readers' Thesaurus
(large print edition)**

For further information or a free brochure, please contact us at:
**Ulverscroft Large Print Books Ltd.,
The Green, Bradgate Road, Anstey,
Leicester, LE7 7FU, England.
Tel:** (00 44) **0116 236 4325
Fax:** (00 44) **0116 234 0205**

CONVALESCENT HEART

Lynne Collins

They called Romily the Snow Queen, but once she had been all fire and passion, kindled into loving by a man's kiss and sure it would last a lifetime. She still believed it would, for her. It had lasted only a few months for the man who had stormed into her heart. After Greg, how could she trust any man again? So was it likely that surgeon Jake Conway could pierce the icy armour that the lovely ward sister had wrapped about her emotions?

TOO MANY LOVES

Juliet Gray

Justin Caldwell, a famous personality of stage and screen, was blessed with good looks and charm that few women could resist. Stacy was a newcomer to England and she was not impressed by the handsome stranger; she thought him arrogant, ill-mannered and detestable. By the time that Justin desired to begin again on a new footing it was much too late to redeem himself in her eyes, for there had been too many loves in his life.

MYSTERY AT MELBECK

Gillian Kaye

Meg Bowering goes to Melbeck House in the Yorkshire Dales to nurse the rich, elderly Mrs Peacock. She likes her patient and is immediately attracted to Mrs Peacock's nephew and heir, Geoffrey, who farms nearby. But Geoffrey is a gambling man and Meg could never have foreseen the dreadful chain of events which follow. Throughout her ordeal, she is helped by the local vicar, Andrew Sheratt, and she soon discovers where her heart really lies.

HEART UNDER SIEGE

Joy St Clair

Gemma had no interest in men — which was how she had acquired the job of companion/secretary to Mrs Prescott in Kentucky. The old lady had stipulated that she wanted someone who would not want to rush off and get married. But why was the infuriating Shade Lambert so sceptical about it? Gemma was determined to prove to him that she meant what she said about remaining single — but all she proved was that she was far from immune to his devastating attraction!